THE
SANDGLASS

O

Romesh Gunesekera

Doubleday Canada Limited

First published in Canada by Doubleday Canada Limited 1998

CANADIAN CATALOGUING IN PUBLICATION DATA

Gunesekera, Romesh
    The sandglass

ISBN 0-385-25812-7

I. Title.

PR9440.9. G86S26 1998 823 C98-931193-7

Printed and bound in the USA

Published in Canada by

Doubleday Canada Limited
105 Bond Street
Toronto, Ontario
M5B 1Y3

NEW 10 9 8 7 6 5 4 3 2 1

For Helen,
for Shanthi and Tanisa

In memory of my father
and
absent friends

No thing can go back to nothing.

Marcus Aurelius

ACKNOWLEDGEMENTS

My thanks to friends and family who have provided me with time and space to write, and to my editors, past and present.

I am also grateful for the luck to have found bookshelves where *The Divine Comedy* could share space with *Stories My Mother Never Told Me*.

CONTENTS

THE DUCALS

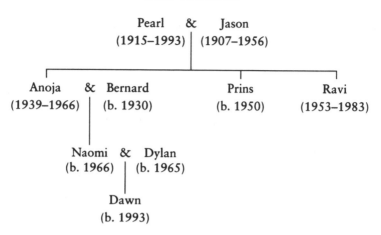

Pearl & Jason
(1915–1993) (1907–1956)

Anoja & Bernard   Prins   Ravi
(1939–1966) (b. 1930)   (b. 1950)   (1953–1983)

Naomi & Dylan
(b. 1966) (b. 1965)

Dawn
(b. 1993)

THE VATUNASES

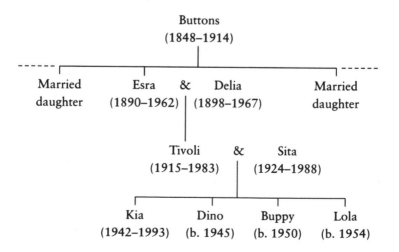

Buttons
(1848–1914)

Married   Esra & Delia   Married
daughter   (1890–1962) (1898–1967)   daughter

Tivoli & Sita
(1915–1983) (1924–1988)

Kia   Dino   Buppy   Lola
(1942–1993) (b. 1945)   (b. 1950)   (b. 1954)

DAYBREAK

Two months after Pearl died I was huddled in a smart-card hotel room on the other side of the world, twenty-five storeys high, watching the gloom of a grey morning settle like ash. Below me a line of grimy white cars, trucks and vans stood gridlocked on a flyover going nowhere. The whole cadaverous city seemed to rise on a tide of rubble.

I felt uneasy: I couldn't concentrate on my surroundings or my work. I was worried about my friend Prins, Pearl's son, whom I had known for seventeen years and now seemed to have gone into hiding in Colombo.

Every time I think of what has happened to Pearl, and what might have happened to Prins, I feel the blood pump in my head.

Prins had sent me an enigmatic message that April, before I left London on a business trip to Tokyo, but I could not reach him anywhere. I decided to stop over in Colombo on my way back. There was nothing else I could think of doing.

In every place I have been to since then, I seem to end up in a low-lit hotel room going over the story of Prins and Pearl – the whole Ducal family and the scheming Vatunases, who seemed forever coiled around them – trying to untangle the truth from the words I found hidden in Pearl's battered biscuit tin, the weatherproof journal of jottings Prins sent me, and the orphaned fragments of my aborted past.

The last time I met Prins was in February that same traumatic year – 1993 – when he returned to London for Pearl's funeral.

I

M O R N I N G

'Is she really dead?' Prins stared at me, his breath wreathing in the frosty air outside my front door.

I clasped his arm and embraced him awkwardly, 'I'm sorry.' His blue shoulders seemed padded with ice. I ushered him in.

He blinked under the hall light.

'You OK?' I didn't know what else to say.

'You know, I took a taxi straight to the crematorium. It was freezing. My mouth was dry. I thought I was late. But, thank God, I could see a crowd still waiting to go in. I headed straight for the middle thinking who are all these *yakkoes*? I didn't recognize a single face around me.' Prins spoke with bewildering speed, clutching the banister in the hallway.

'Why suddenly swoop here, all making the place even

3

grimmer with those dark polypropylene half-wool winter coats? Those heaps of shapeless bloody Kashmir shrouds. They were beginning to stir with anticipation, but I kept thinking: Where is Chip – you? Or anyone I might know? What has been going on these last dozen years? What the hell has the old girl been up to? Reviving Sheba's court?' He widened his eyes in disbelief. 'Then this small man with gold spectacles tugs my sleeve, "Excuse me, are you friend or relative?"

'"Relative," I say. "I am the son, Prins."

'The fellow jumps back, startled. "Oh, I see." He looks around for help but by then the whole bloody crowd has vanished. "The other relatives are inside," he stammers, "but nobody said anything about Dr Viswanathan's son . . ."'

Prins shoved his big hand up in the air. '"Who the hell is Dr Viswanathan?" And the fellow whispers, "the deceased."

'"What about my mother?"

'"Your mother?" he says.

'"Jesus bloody Christ! Where is my mother? She is meant to be here. Dead. What the hell is going on?"

'Next second the bugger had bolted into the crematorium like someone had lit a fuse up his arse.' Prins shook his head from side to side in exasperation.

'There I am, hatless, tieless, coatless, frigorific in the *pol-* polar wind and surrounded by a forest of bare bloody saplings commemorating everyone in London but her. I felt like a damn fool. The whole thing seemed a stupid joke. And if it was true, maybe I should have gone to the cemetery in Colombo – Kanatta – by the golf course and meditated. Or played putt. Or just got plastered.'

'But the funeral is not until Friday,' I managed to interject.

'So I discovered, but on Naomi's fax the 19 looked like a 17. Today.' He glared defiantly.

'The funeral will be on the *19th*,' I confirmed. 'Friday at nine o'clock.'

'I know. I've got to fly back the same night.'

Prins had tried calling Naomi, his niece, at his mother's flat several times but there had been no answer. The first fax she had sent about Pearl's death was indecipherable and the second, with the date of the funeral, was smudged and had no reply number. He had tried to get hold of me but my answering machine had run out of tape. He had to work out what had happened. It had been a rush then to catch a plane in time. He had tried Naomi again from the cemetery but had had no success. 'As your phone was now engaged I reckoned you, at least, must be home.'

I said I was between assignments. I didn't say I had been calling my office to extend my leave because I couldn't face going back to work so soon after Pearl's death. 'Anyway, you're here now.'

He peered at the mirror on the wall next to him. 'It was a hellava journey – all the direct flights were fully booked – but I managed to get into a VIP lounge at the last stop: you can get really spruced up in those, you know. Shit, shave and shower all in one go. But the damn tie, I lost.' He pulled at the collar under his long jaw. He still had the face of an agitated ram, but he'd become greyer in the two years since I'd last seen him. That was in Sri Lanka, in 1991, the first time I had been back since I came to England. Prins had gone back to live there nearly ten years earlier when he'd chucked his striped shirts and kitsch-links in a black bin-liner for Oxfam and set off to find his true self in the sun. 'My destiny is not in this place,' he had grumbled, aping Marlon Brando. It was easy in those days to have heroes who were not like us, to borrow icons even as we smashed our own. Now with about every tenth hair turned silver he looked as if he lived permanently under moonlight. But his gaberdine blazer and brushed-cotton trousers, with their fine glacial sheen, made him look as though he was going yachting in the Mediterranean instead of to his mother's funeral; the outfit was the warmest he could find at home.

'I feel so cold and hungry. Everything is almost out-of-control, you know. Like I've misread the road signs but not quite let go of the wheel.' Prins moved his hands on an imaginary steering wheel. 'What'll happen if I go *hirivatuna* and let go?' A shiver shook his body as he stretched, tilting his face: a misbegotten coconut tree in search of the sun.

'Where's your stuff? Don't you have a suitcase or anything?'

'We are very modern in Colombo now, you know: carry only plastic – like our smart-ass politicos. Otherwise they think you are packing a bomb.' All he had was a small black bag on his shoulder which I hadn't even noticed before. 'I knew I'd have to dash for a taxi and go straight to the crematorium. Couldn't lug a suitcase there anyway, could I?'

o

I took Prins into the kitchen and gave him a bowl of bran muesli. Wednesday morning, ten o'clock. Simon & Garfunkel were on the radio. I made coffee. Prins said he felt as if he was back in his mother's kitchen twelve years ago: golden oldies, Pearl pouring coffee. But the Pearl he remembered was rather different from the one I had come to know.

I felt a little apprehensive. I didn't know how Prins would react to me now, back in London: to my closeness to Pearl, made possible only by his absence, by my not being one of her children, perhaps by my not having a mother to call on. But I was the one who was there, willing to share the reality of her words and peek into another world.

On the side of the dresser behind him, above the telephone, I had pinned my only photograph of Pearl. A snapshot from before I was born. I had never got round to framing it properly. A drift of mauvish fluff and dust had collected on the curled-up corners. I wiped the photograph on my sleeve and slipped it into the drawer underneath the stack of telephone directories.

II

TEN O'CLOCK

I first met Pearl when I came to London in the autumn of 1975.

I had left Sri Lanka some years before but still had no place of my own. Not having a job at the time, I had borrowed some money and travelled to London determined to live out what was perhaps a misplaced but youthful dream. Staying with Pearl, at 52b Almeida Avenue, made it possible. She had a spare room because Prins – her elder son – had gone to Oldham on a ten-month stint learning to sell woollen yarn. His younger brother, Ravi, was living with Pearl but he tended to lock himself away in the darkest bedroom of the flat.

Most evenings during that first cold year I would sit on a brown leatherette armchair opposite Pearl, sipping sherry and listening to her stories, while she knitted shawls or cardigans on the sofa, between scenes of vintage movies and episodes of *Kojak* on TV. Even then I was looking for a way to shape my life in the wake of her own effervescent trail. Pearl, then Prins, became the cardinal points for my uncertain identity.

'The trouble started when he got that tomfool idea into his head about owning a house,' Pearl put down her knitting needles and patted her lips lightly, as if to coax out one of the mischievous phrases with which she used to mock the priggish English of her childhood. 'What for owning an inchy-pinchy graveyard, I ask you? But that man was so desperate for his own dung heap, he thought of nothing else.'

He was her husband, Jason Ducal.

Pearl would recount the story of those early days with such candour that I felt I was there with her, an invisible eavesdropper in the twilight of a camphoric age.

o

Pearl had been brought up almost in quarantine, in houses with acres of empty space; but they were never houses owned by her parents. Her father, a doctor, had moved from place to place trying to give help wherever it was needed. He had died in the malaria epidemic of 1935. Her mother had been a victim of the disease earlier, but Pearl never spoke about her – except to give me her name, Sikata, and say that as a result her father always found a house with clean sea or mountain air for his only child. Pearl grew up revelling in *Father Brown* mysteries and English romances under mango trees in secluded gardens. Other people entered her world only through the surgery door: vulnerable, hurt people seeking a bit of help in their struggle to survive from one day to the next.

That was why Jason had seemed so fascinating when he arrived at their house. He had no obvious afflictions or injuries. 'He didn't look ill,' she would say with real surprise in her voice. He rode a bicycle and acted as though he belonged in a Russian play. He would arrive riding with just one finger on the handlebar and a flower in his other hand. While his contemporaries swotted night and day for their future status in a ramshackle empire, Jason spoke enchantingly about the need for beauty, and the transmigration of souls. 'But there was never any *boru-part* about him, you know. I have to say.' Pearl would shake her head in admiration, even after all these years. 'No, not in those early days. Never, I guess. He was sincere. He didn't put on airs like the rest of them,' she sighed. She was young then. She had believed in Jason and his sparkling bicycle, his neatly plucked flower, his deliciously heady words. She married him for romance, she said, but Jason, it seems, quickly came to feel that he needed to replenish her world with the accoutrements of her late father's home: a sideboard, bookshelves, a garden, rather than simply with a good doctor's flair.

All the months of their courtship he had been so debonair. 'He'd recite poems to me, you know, *real* poems. And sometimes we would walk together in the evening by the sea and he would tell me about the stars and Venus, "The eye of love in the sky".' She had been impressed by the way he could brush away the cares of the world and simply look into her face; enter her almost, through her eyes, like a smile lodged somewhere between her throat and her heart. But that ability to be inside her without even touching her had disappeared after the wedding, as if physically entering her that first night made it impossible for him to ever reach her any other way. Pearl was concerned that she did not become pregnant immediately, in the way that she had been led to expect by her father's abbreviated biology lessons. 'I felt it was my fault that it had not happened right away,' she giggled, 'some instinctive technique which I missed out, you know, that would have released an egg like a *ping* ball, at the same-same instant that he *sprung* his sperm.' Jason had seemed disillusioned.

Each successive day after the wedding he became more

and more obsessed with finding something that would launch their lives into a richer orbit. He ridiculed the examination system for public service and bemoaned his lost opportunities with the professions. He became determined to break the mould and breach Colombo's foreign mercantile sector. All signs of levity evaporated. 'You'd think our wedding had triggered a mission.' She couldn't understand the transformation. 'What was this urge? I used to ask myself, this urge to go out? Why was he not there with me all the time, while I was still in such a state over my father's death?' Pearl would look at me as if the answer was lodged in my head. But she was the one who knew everything, not me. Jason Ducal was a man of no means. Although Pearl's father had provided for her, before donating the rest of his small estate to a hospice, Jason had no money of his own. And, after his marriage, this seemed to have troubled him greatly.

O

Before the end of their first year of marriage, in 1936, Jason had secured a unique position with Sanderson Bros., a relatively new British firm in Colombo dealing with tea, shipping and the regular cosseting of an ageing empire. It was a coup. No Ceylonese had ever before penetrated this last bastion of British colonial conservatism, not at the level he did. 'The only *brownskins* before him had been peons and clerks,' Pearl sniffed. The firm, at the time, was exceptionally prescient; it recognized the need to ride the wave of nationalism sweeping the island and develop local managers, cultivate the indigenous elite and turn itself into a genuine Ceylonese entity before the inevitable transfer of power. While other British firms rubbished all talk of Ceylonization, Sanderson Bros. had cautiously welcomed the idea; they were prepared to experiment. Jason convinced the senior partners that he was the man who would show them the future and they appointed him to an executive position that baffled all the gazetteers of the annual Ceylon Directory. '"Who is this squirt?" The planters at the Hill Club were thoroughly miffed,' Pearl added with pleasure. But neither Jason nor Pearl quite realized how much of a turning point his appointment would prove to be.

'He was grinning like mad, the day he got that job. I don't know what he did to get it, but he could pour on the charm when he wanted to back then.' Pearl sucked in her lips, hiding them in her mouth. 'I was happy to see him happy, but when I tried to kiss him, he pulled away. He wanted to talk. It was the last time he really wanted to talk. He hadn't even got to the office yet, and already he was dreaming of his house. "A proper house of our own, with a garden," you know.'

'They gave a house?' I asked.

'No, not like that. He was the first *kaluwa*, no? In those firms only the British were *given* houses. But he saw how one day owning a house might be possible for folk like us. His face was so bright with hope. He was determined to make it on his own, unlike all those other Colombo dimbats with their creepy ancestors and shady money.'

Jason proved to be an extraordinary success at the firm. He quickly rose to a position which involved him in frequent excursions around the island. 'He was invaluable to the Raj-barge who didn't know what to do about all the Trades Union business and the new politics. So while that Bracegirdle chappie, the Commie, was fighting against deportation to Australia in that famous case before the war, Jason put in for a passage to England and got it.' But the travel was, as always, two-edged. On the one hand his absence put their home on a precipice; on the other hand Pearl was able to go with him. The trip to England changed her life forever. She loved to talk about that journey as though it was the true culmination of their earlier courtship.

There is only one photograph of the two of them *together* from that time. On the back is the caption '1938' and below that, rather more meticulously, 'Jason & Pearl'. Pearl is looking at Jason, but Jason is looking straight into the camera lens like a slightly camp model. Displayed in his hand is an envelope emblazoned with the words 'AIR MAIL', the latest postal service, presumably with the details of their tour abroad. Pearl first told me about that trip after we watched *The Thirty-Nine Steps* on TV. She had come with Jason by ship to spend two months in England and Scotland early in the summer of 1938. 'We took a train just like Hannay, but Scotland was nothing like as bleak as they made it look. It was wonderful. Iain met us at the other end and took us around.'

'They filmed it in Ireland pretending it was Scotland – a bit of Hitchcock's artistic licence plus the usual financial motive,' I offered as justification. 'Who was Iain?'

'Iain Stevenson. A senior partner. Jason was his protégé. He was on furlough also. Imagine us on *furlough*. Pretending to go home from home. But Iain was a wonderful, kind man. He was the one who gave Jason a taste for real malt whisky. He took us to his favourite distillery on Speyside. Jason loved it: the idea of being a connoisseur or whatever. And then there was the golf.'

He had taken them to St Andrews. 'I got a birdie,' Pearl beamed. 'At that stage I was a better golfer than Jason, you know. He was as jerky as a chicken wing; his swing was flatter than a Bambalapitiya cheesecake. But I gave it up because he would get so upset. Iain taught him first, and he taught me just for fun.'

'You gave up?' I couldn't imagine Pearl giving anything up without a fight.

She turned away and looked out through the summer-glazed windows freckled with the soft grey rain she was so fond of. 'They wanted to be champions, you know. Always playing the boys' game. Later we had Ladies' sections and all, but to tell you the truth, I found the clubby life back home a little vulgar. Non-stop innuendo.' I could imagine the belly laughs, the loud jokes about improbably high arcs sprinkling the greens. 'Iain was the only real gentleman out of that rum lot.'

Iain Stevenson came from Aberdeen, but had lived in Ceylon for more than half his life. 'He had a lovely face,' Pearl said. The skin around his eyes was crinkly as though he was smiling all the time. The effect of twenty years of squinting against the sun, measuring a shadow as it tried to break away from the past. 'He loved golf. He played it almost every day. Any time he was within striking distance of some kind of a course. Sometimes a handful of holes dotted around a Mahawamsa ruin, with anthills for bunkers and bathing ponds for water hazards. Sometimes just the potted garden of the GA – the Government Agent. Golf was like a religion for him,' Pearl explained.

Iain Stevenson had lent Jason his sports car so that they could see more of his native Scotland and then take their time driving back to London. It was a summer of gathering clouds in Europe, but for Pearl it seemed to have been a rare moment of bliss. 'We had a *hoot*,' Pearl would chuckle. 'Jason loved that Triumph. We would go topless – no roof you understand – come rain or shine.'

'What, getting wet?'

'It was a Triumph, Chip *putha*,' Pearl whistled, 'we'd go like the wind.'

For my birthday she gave me one of the photographs from that trip in 1938. 'Here,' she peeled it out of the album. 'You are the only one who likes looking at these now.' There were about thirty photographs meticulously mounted with silver corners. All taken by Jason. The one Pearl gave me is of her sitting in the open roadster, looking a little grumpy despite the attention that Jason seems to be lavishing on her from behind the lens. Pearl looks as if she wants to smile, to beam back, but a small doubt in her mind has cut the threads to her cheeks. Perhaps it was the car that Jason adored. You could see she couldn't tell. Jason, she seemed to be insisting, tell me you love me. Jason was always handling the camera and seems to have fancied himself as an artist. There were no photos of him from that trip. His only image was the imprint of his eye; the frame he wrapped around the world of his Triumph, his young wife, and his pleasure.

'That was near Hyde Park, I think. We had been to see the horses on Rotten Row. In the evening, I remember, he bought me roses. We had dinner at Simpsons where I wore my fanciest Manipuri sari.' In her yellow Almeida Avenue sitting room Pearl loved to describe this exotic past of hers to me as though it were the ordinary precursor to any immigrant life. Always bright and brimful with none of the sooty drabness offered by the sourer reflections of those times.

'It was before that Munich, you know,' she would say as if hers had been an innocent world. She never had to face the true terrors of war, but even so her world gained its own sorrows. Experience more sober, more sombre. Tougher. Harder. Poorer. Sadder than she could ever have expected. But when she spoke, it seemed as though she felt life could be controlled to run in certain patterns whatever its trials. As though when life was going downhill it was only gathering speed for some stupendous leap to come. A life after Jason.

I asked her what had happened to Iain Stevenson. 'Did he stay on?'

'Scotland was the place he dreamed about. He left Colombo and came back here in the fifties.'

'Is he still around?'

'No,' she shook her head wistfully. 'He died in a terrible accident by Loch Linnhe. He had just bought a beautiful brand new blue MG.'

I asked her when that had happened.

'Oh, long ago. That was in 1957. A year after Jason. You would have been just a boy.'

○

Pearl's first child, Prins's sister Anoja, was born prematurely. Pearl said she was sure the baby was conceived on the ship the night before they slid back into Colombo harbour. 'I got the technique right when I heard the Captain talk about berth lamps.' Pearl looked at me out of the corner of her eye, ready to burst out laughing. She must have kicked her husband in harder than ever before that last night, right up into her womb, to make the difference. 'It seemed so right, to come back bearing the ultimate wedding gift, even if it *was* only a gift for me. A loan.' Pearl's expression changed and a slight tremor touched her lower lip.

'But, you know, Anoja was never a happy child. Even as a baby she was so droopy. Jason would complain her eyes were so *unknowing*. That she never smiled.' Anoja seemed to have made Jason curiously unhappy in those early years, despite his growing commercial success. Perhaps because he felt helpless against the sorrow of the world that would seep into her new life and drown its innocence.

'But *he* wouldn't smile either,' Pearl complained. 'I kept

telling him, Don't frighten the baba with that *guli-guli* look of yours.'

In her first years, the baby – Anoja – would spend most of her time on her own or with a succession of gloomy, wizened ayahs. Each introducing an even darker sense of doom and desperation from their own doleful lives into her precarious existence. 'You know, Chip *putha*, I was so young in those days. I just let her grow. She didn't make any fuss, you see. She was happy to jus' be. And I was so preoccupied with what was happening to my Jason: the transformation of the man.'

Jason put all his energy into his work. He was promoted swiftly to fill the vacancies left by the more disillusioned British executives in the firm who could not understand the need for any form of Ceylonization. The ones who preferred to return to a Britain stumbling from financial crisis to war than oversee a loss of what Pearl called their 'prissy privileges'. Every month when Jason came back from touring the estates in the hill country he would find he had been given new responsibilities, and risen higher up the firm. 'The colour ceilings, bars and walls' – as Pearl quipped – crumbled in the face of the need to fill vacancies quickly against local competitors. With each change came more travel and more involvement for Jason; more distance from Pearl and Anoja. But all the time the possibility of buying his own dream-house was also becoming more real.

Throughout the war years the firm was quietly overhauled; by the time of full national Independence, Sanderson Bros. had been completely reformed and had a Board of a different hue, completely confounding the ideas of commercial identity – what made a firm the same when practically everything about it had changed? – hitherto accepted as the norm in the comfortable mercantilist society of a colonial island.

○

Then, in the heady rush of 1948, while the pundits argued about the colours of a free flag, Jason Ducal bought a house where no Ducal before him had ever dreamed of owning one. It was in one of the more desirable parts of Colombo. 'But,' Pearl wrinkled up her nose, 'the only problem was that it bordered the land of the Vatunas family.'

The land of the Vatunases was the result of a deep and intense relationship between the sleeping earth and the ambitions of a line of modern dynasts. And for the Vatunases, from the first to the last, land defined everything: the shape of their lives, the shape of their bodies and their heads and the shape of their dreams. Jason did not realize it at first – he was too unknowing – but in purchasing this house he was buying into a form of destiny that would infect his own life and that of all the Ducals, including Pearl, her daughter Anoja, and her sons Ravi and Prins, with the disease of the landed.

'Funnily enough the house he bought had belonged to an Englishman, you know. The land itself was originally plain old Vatunas land, but the plot had been sold to one Captain Melrose who then built the house. He called it Arcadia.' Pearl said that Captain Melrose had always been regarded as eccentric even among his own people and had built the house as a kind of homage to a suppurating colonial dream: the dream of a voyage of adventure. The way she described it, the master bedroom seemed to lie at one end, close to the road, as if in the forecastle of an amphibian slouching towards the sea. A Captain's study had been built above it with a ship's bridge which served as a balcony. 'The whole of the rest of the house went glug-glug-glug down from there.' A magnified tear.

'Jason loved that wretched house.' Pearl plucked at some stray wool on her lap. 'He loved going up to the bridge early in the evening; feeling that he was high and still rising, up to his hidey-hole of rejuvenating dreams. A place of no vail. The day could be left behind him and he could find a centre to his sense of himself.' Jason seemed to have become a true colonial: a man obsessed with place and status – geographical and social. Only once assured of his own place in the murkiness of the universe could he bring order and shape to life around him. Without him, he seemed to believe, there would be no order. Nothing would work. Pearl also seemed to subscribe to this view of the world. 'For him to work his magic, he needed the boost of a couple of hops upwards to a place of his own.'

From her words I formed a picture of his study: *a vast wicker chair, sensations settling down like motes in sea-ionized air. Jason closing his eyes to calm the chemical and molecular agitation of his heart. The sound of the town receding and his ears filling with the hiss of his own being; the planes of light and substance melting, and slowly the shape of his life condensing into the mood of the present. Then, when it was clear to him that all was well, Jason would emerge refreshed.*

'No one else was ever allowed to pry up there,' Pearl frowned at the recollection. 'One time a cousin of Jason's came with a young boy, Baresh, who was mad about ships. He had a sailor's cap. The father was quite excited about Jason's ridiculous house and let the little fellow run upstairs to the bridge. Jason got into such a state he almost threw the little boy down the stairs. But Baresh came back, you know, like a cork, when he was older. But by then it was on account of Anoja.'

I could see Pearl as a young mother: *She is on the veranda brushing her first-born daughter's hair, watching the air turn to metal in the dying sun. She sinks her nose into her child's hair to breathe in the heat of her life and to hope for luck.*

'There was something really very queery about that house. I could sense his need for it, but I could not share it. The whole garden felt creepy, as if the edges harboured something malign.'

She said she felt reluctant to challenge Jason's well-being with her unease, but she knew she did not want to die in this house of his. 'I could feel something pushing me or pulling me out of his Arcadia. But looking at Jason, I could see that he felt the opposite. He wanted that house to be his whole life: the place where *he* would die.' The incompatibility still disturbed her.

'I don't know what I saw. Sometimes I feel I have blundered so many times, nothing matters any more. But how Jason became such a success in that firm is a mystery to me. I never expected him to become anything like that. He was so full of books. He talked about Coriolanus and the myth of Sisyphus. For me he had something of Mr Jeyaratnam about him, the only man-teacher I ever had. But that job at Sanderson Bros. changed everything. No more bicycle, no more books. Only his work, which he hid behind closed doors. Always shutting doors, closing things. It began to get on my nerves, actually.'

The scene unfolded in my mind. *A Friday evening, in the hottest month of the year: Jason is closing the bedroom door after his bath. Pearl waiting on the Veranda, starts.*

'Why shut that rickety-tick door?'

Jason stops and looks at her.

'Always you are closing doors. Like shutting me out, no?'

Jason turns away. He rubs one of his eyebrows slowly. 'It's hot,' he mumbles.

'So what?'

'In the evening the heat comes in. I'm just keeping the room cool.'

'Don't be such a dum-dum.'

Jason gazes out at the garden. 'It's true. Can't you feel it? The heat coming off the road?'

Pearl looks steadily at Jason as if waiting for his eyes to return to her. 'I feel hardly anything nowadays,' she says. 'Nothing moves here. It's a graveyard. I need to get out.'

Their eyes meet briefly, before Jason manages to pull his away. He does not reply. Instead, he walks down the steps into the small driveway. Pearl watches her husband grow darker as the light fails outside. The sky turns luminous for a moment, before oxidizing in the ill wind. The air is dank enough to choke on.

'Sweetheart,' he had once murmured, his skin warm and pulsing, his breath in her heart: 'Sweetheart.' But now the whistling sound of those syllables seems to fly from the trees and bushes like owls and fruit bats chasing contorted shadows. Shrill in her ears, as though he himself is scream-

ing with the deformed night creatures in his heart, although
he says nothing and seems as still as a rock.

Tell me, she says to herself. Tell me, tell me, tell me why.
Why so distant? Where are you?

Arcadia was meant to bring them closer together; it was
Jason's dream of a family home. But it came as a surprise to
Pearl. She was not involved in the decision to buy it. Jason
had become used to running things by himself by then:
managing offices, a company, people. He was a businessman of a new age. He bought the house and then brought
his family into it. It had seemed perfectly simple. Pearl
knew nothing about the trouble he had had with old Esra
Vatunas over the purchase, not until they moved in.

o

'Our biggest problem was the shape of the land itself.' Pearl
used her knitting needle as a pointer. Arcadia was almost
circumscribed by the territory of the Vatunases: a pebble in
the fist of Esra Vatunas.

Esra's father, Buttons Vatunas, had originally acquired a
large tract of residential land in the 1880s and built a man-
sion – Bellevue – near the centre. But then he had the
bizarre idea of using his family tree to make procreative

sculptures out of his property, and deliberately set about carving his estate into peculiar shapes for his children. He wanted testicles for one, a vulva for another, a lingam for a third, swollen glans and so on. His early wills were a whirligig of reproductive drawings. He had six children, three of whom died before he did, and with each death his lewd land-map was modified until it became almost completely illegible. In the end he found that he had two ungracious daughters, a problem son and a map that looked like a precursor to an erotic Picasso. The daughters quickly selected husbands in the course of their first season at Colombo's then grand races and end-of-the-century balls, tame trailers to the manic millennium frenzy to come, and the old man had to give two pieces of his precious land to them before he was ready. Because he thought that their high-collar husbands were out-of-pocket money-grabbers, he simplified his dynastic map and made their land into wasp-waisted hourglass strips pushed apart by a bulging block in the centre for his only surviving son.

Then, just before he died, Buttons came to the conclusion that his son Esra was a scoundrel. Legend has it that Buttons had moaned 'Arsehole' at the mention of Esra's name when reviewing his last will and testament. But Esra was the sole son, the only one who would carry on the eccentric family name. Buttons decided he had to let Esra gain his juicy inheritance, but he ensured that it had a hole punctured in the appropriate place: a *vala* to be remembered by, much deeper than a tomb. Before he died, Buttons sold a chunk of the central block of land to Captain Melrose. Esra was left with the remainder: a sharp, crescent-shaped piece with a stately house in the middle and a curved lane leading up to it, then out, and somebody else's property on the rim where there should have been an ample Lancelot Brown garden with lusty frills and lovely deceptions. But Esra, the son, was a resourceful scoundrel. He quickly learned to see the shape of his land itself as its virtue; he described his property as the imprint of a divine hoof as God cantered to heaven from the island, neatly obscuring the secret lasciviousness of his father's vision.

'The old goat was mostly irritated by the fact that there was a Britisher like a wasp in a honey pot in what should have been his garden.' Pearl would cackle at the picture she painted of Captain Melrose marooned between Esra's twin horns of avarice and adversity. 'Thirty years before we turned up Esra was already lining the drive with prickly pears and hornets' nests; he had gardeners feed monstrous plants with the choicest, steaming, horse manure every month and burn garden rubbish in a ring of fire around Arcadia.' But the smoke, the ash, the smell of horse shit all affected Bellevue as much as Arcadia, and the border grew more luscious with every attack.

Esra Vatunas's only real satisfaction in his battle with

Melrose was in outliving two generations of the enemy. He gloated over Captain Melrose's impotent family thinning out to a nephew and then finally to young Maurice Melrose who in 1948, with the independence of the island declared and the war in Europe, Africa and Asia over, decided to sell up his imperial holdings and return to his subterranean roots. Maurice had some expectation that Fitzrovia in London might become what Berlin had been before the war and preferred to be there rather than in the doldrums of Eden.

The moment Esra Vatunas heard about the imminent sale of what had become an ulcer in the land of the Vatunases, he offered a large pot of money to Maurice. But the young man was loyal enough to the memory of old Captain Melrose to insist that Arcadia go to anyone but a Vatunas. When the offer was rejected, Esra tried subterfuge and sent a dhobi in disguise to buy it on his behalf. When that failed, he started a campaign of sorcery – burying shrunken skulls and boiled semen behind the culvert between the houses – to bewitch the place and scare off any prospective local buyers.

Then Jason appeared. He turned out to be in the right place at the right time. Or, as Pearl would put it, in the wrong place at the wrong time with too much money to escape. When Esra heard that Jason Ducal had secured the property, he wrote to Jason offering to double his money by an immediate resale. But Jason had been warned by Maurice of the odd neighbour at the bottom of the garden, and Esra Vatunas was notorious for his sharp dealings and ability to succeed always at somebody else's expense. Jason ignored the lucrative offer. Esra became even angrier over this rebuff than over the twenty-four years of foreign occupation, and a renewed campaign of attrition ensued: smears, sneers and ever more horse shit was piled around Arcadia and its newly arrived inhabitants.

○

'Esra Vatunas was a wickedly wealthy old man.' Pearl's tone of voice implied that a wholesome blend of morals and money was impossible given the nature of the human species. I asked her how the Vatunases had become so prosperous. 'Buttons was the one,' she rummaged around her knitting basket for her needles. 'Shrewd as a monkey's uncle and something of a lech, but he had a bit of glamour and all the luck in the world.' Buttons Vatunas had bought into coconut land and cinnamon from the profits of a gem pit discovered on a tiny plot of land wangled in his youth, and then leaped unerringly from coffee to tea and urban property in the land-grabs of the 1880s. Buttons's switch from coffee to tea was seen by his cronies as sheer brilliance and socially useful: neatly undermining the dominance of British planters and reorienting the country's talents and the whole economy towards tea and tiffin. Buttons's commercial rewards came with the boom years and were considered by his fellow entrepreneurs as the proper fruits of his remarkable efforts. Only later, when a new generation of economists began to talk of development, did his enterprise become condemned as, at best, a mistake and, at worst, diabolical for forcing the yoke of plantation servitude upon a once proud and sovereign land.

But Esra, his son, was seen by *everyone* as a much more rapacious predator. 'Esra had no glamour but he had a double dose of shrewdness. I think he went into rubber and fertilizers.' Pearl looked up over her yarn as if Esra had suddenly walked into the room. 'He always looked so hungry. Rich men don't usually look starving, no? But this one did. His eyes devoured everything in front of him. Gaunt and bony, like he was sucking the life out of the whole world. He had neat – quite tiny – teeth and there seemed to be more of them than in any normal mouth. Always clickety-clicking.' Pearl demonstrated with her needles in fast knit.

'His wife, Delia, was not so bad. At least she tried to talk to me after Jason died. But she was another suspiciously slim one: small feet, small pelvis. She gave birth only once, they say, with great pain and agony.' After she produced her son, Tivoli, she had howled, 'Not another one ever', and Esra, despite his rabid Vatunas genes, had to 'button up', Pearl joked.

o

Tivoli, according to Pearl, showed no sign of the voracious appetite of the earlier Vatunases. She spoke quite warmly of him – the new Vatunas. 'As a child, they say, he could not have been a bigger disappointment to that slippery warlock Esra: he seemed placid to the point of inertia. But he was a dreamer for a long time, you see, like Jason was at first.' From an early age he turned in on himself and showed no interest in the Vatunas plots that Esra puffed over. All he ever seemed to do was doodle on scraps of paper.

'Esra could not speak to Tivoli without ridiculing him,' Pearl said sadly. 'Sarcasm and irony became their only kind of talk when they came across each other in that monstrous house.' Father and son both painfully conscious of the fact that the other was always a devastating source of despondency.

Tivoli learned to neglect everything his father might

want him to pursue. He did appallingly at school; ignored the prospect of higher or further education; he took no interest in coconut, tea, rubber or fertilizer and seemed to regard Bellevue as a penitentiary. When in 1940 his aunt Rosa, Esra's childless sister on the right of the Vatunas crescent, killed herself and her husband because of an affair he was having with the second cousin of a prominent Marxist, leaving Tivoli as her heir, he immediately moved out of Esra's house into his own wasp-waisted tract of Vatunas land. Eight years before Jason bought Arcadia, Tivoli was installed in his own house on the other side of the lane.

'"What have you produced?" Esra used to complain to his wife. "Does this boy have a poker, or only a bleeding pencil?" He would shout at Delia, clicking his teeth like mad. "Get the fellow a wife,"' Pearl tittered as she put on the different voices. '"He needs to do something besides sit on his backside doodling all day. Get him to pull his socks up. Let him at least produce a grandson for us. Do it soon, before the fellow turns peculiar, you know." Prim little Delia would refuse to be ruffled. "What for, so much trouble? What makes you think that a grandchild would make any difference? You never loved him." But Esra was cruel and crass. "It's not love, you stupid woman. It's the blooming future. Can't you see?" The horrible little gnome was obsessed with the destiny of the Vatunas dynasty.'

'Our future hangs in his balls,' I could imagine the whole neighbourhood echo with Esra's thunder.

○

'Tivoli's mother was the one who pushed him into his marriage. "This Sita, darling, is a very nice girl. You will like her,"' Pearl mimicked. 'Delia was completely enveloped by the myth-making of the Vatunases,' Pearl claimed. 'She worked as hard as any Vatunas to be a snooty breeder rather than just a moneymaker. But her Tivoli was a shy twenty-six-year-old darling and feigned indifference. Delia cajoled him no end: "You know, it will be nice to have a female here. This house really needs it. Of course I can still send you your seer-fish *ambul thihal* whenever you want, but I think this Sita will be very good for you. She comes from a good professional family. A clean, sensible girl. Perfect for you."'

Tivoli and Sita were married in 1941. A year later they had their first son. Sita was more enamoured with her baby than with her husband. Tivoli saw fatherhood only in terms of his own father's mocking figure, in Bellevue, but now found an equally unpalatable situation growing in his own house where he was having to become a father while he still had difficulties being a son. 'Sita bloomed from a slender,

young, shy, *clean* girl into a soft, big mother very quickly.'
Pearl plumped up the shawl she was knitting. 'But the baby
popping out of her seemed, to Tivoli, to turn Sita inside out.
He never liked babies, you see. To him she, as the mother of
his children, no longer had an inner life; everything was
now on the outside. He acted as though she could keep
nothing in: no secrets, no private thoughts, no sense of the
past, no dreams of the future. It was all laid out on the
dinner table – from the baby's bottom to the ice cream.
Baba, baba, baba, all the time.' Pearl gabbled, holding her
knitting to her throat like a bib and wobbling her head.

'Sita pampered her baby; oiled it and buttered it and
cuddled it and coddled it for three years until the baby
seemed to turn into a complicated little boy – Kia – at
which point she bloomed again into another pregnancy and
produced Dino, the precocious second son, and a few years
later, Buppy, the third. And then, finally, in a break with the
Vatunas tradition, Lola, her only daughter.'

After the arrival of his grandchildren Esra began to
loosen up. He would get slightly drunk and sit around
Bellevue with a smirk ripening his face. He was delighted to
see the baby penises of his first three grandsons budding out
of the Vatunas lingam stem in such quick succession. He
could see his father's precious family tree, grand and bushy,
fruiting in perpetuity. But Tivoli, like Jason, watched this
sprouting like a completely detached observer in his own

house. The babies grew into Vatunas children. The lines of diapers, baby talk and ancestry were strengthened between his house and his mother's veranda in Bellevue, but Tivoli maintained his distance from the big house. This seems to have been the time he started his wanderlust; straying from Sita's steadily fattening legs.

'You see, his house, like Bellevue, became a black hole for Tivoli. There was nothing for him there inside that perimeter of red hell-fire crotons,' Pearl mused. 'When Tivoli first moved to his own place, he would have seen young Maurice Melrose from his upstairs balcony. He wanted to show even Maurice that all Vatunases were not like Esra, but he found it impossible. Maurice Melrose would have assumed Tivoli was yet another fiendish Vatunas trying to close the circle around him. He would not have known of the gap between father and son. But when we arrived, Tivoli felt a new start might be possible. We did not carry the baggage of a previous generation's enmity. When the sound of his wife and children's babble became too much for him, I would see Tivoli on his balcony dreaming of a way out. We both, for different reasons, felt trapped in that place. We had to do something.'

As Prins would put it, 'You have to escape and go where you can find yourself, or you stay and transform what is around you until it becomes your own.' Except that for Prins, Tivoli was just a wanker who scribbled steamy love sonnets and drew wild pictures of labial passages and phallic wands until his mother, Delia, put him out to rut.

○

After Jason died, Pearl escaped to England. Prins reckoned that she wanted to live in London because it was where she went for her belated honeymoon; the place where she was most in love. 'But who can live forever in a hotel, even a honeymoon hotel?' Prins had fumed once after a row with her over his plan to get a mortgage for a more modern flat for them to live in.

When Pearl had first moved to England Prins was left behind, together with his younger brother Ravi, and his older sister Anoja. They were looked after by Pearl's aunt – who had cared for their mother in the months before she married Jason, just after her father's death. Pearl lived in England for almost two years before bringing Anoja and Ravi over. The months on her own were mysterious. Lost. Perhaps she communed with her deeper self, relived her visit with Jason, before finally establishing a controlled-rent home of her own. All she ever said to me about that time was that she needed to escape from what had happened, but that she had not realized how much money she would need to be free. 'I saw the top and the bottom of the barrel, you know. It turned out I was more alone than I ever knew.'

It was 1966 and Prins was sixteen before he eventually came to England to join her. He was the last and he never forgave her for abandoning him. Once he arrived in England his adolescent rage found its target in Pearl, a mother reclaiming her next child as she lost the first.

Prins never understood Pearl's scheme for the slow exodus of her children. Perhaps it was simply the quirks of immigration, a shortage of cash, the necessary passage of time, but it now seems as though she was fastening each thread of her life to each new mooring point she unearthed, individually, before trying to knit them together into one entity. She never quite managed to keep them all together. Always one or another was unravelling.

O

The Pearl I knew had been ill for years, ever since Prins left, even though to me she simply seemed herself. She never aged in my eyes; she had always been old. But more recently she seemed to be slipping into a hole. There was nothing anyone could do about that. As far as we knew,

39

there was no *one* thing wrong. She was simply collapsing faster than the rest of us. Ahead of the game. Her eyes were not good; glaucoma had narrowed her sight so that she could only see what was in her direct line of vision. Things with light in them she saw best: the television screen, ripe strawberries. 'Angels,' she said. 'The halos, I could see their halos if only they could get their backsides through that door. The door is too stiff. Can you fix it? I can see anything, if it is light. Lightness, you know, is everything.'

'But what about these black cherries?' I once asked. 'How do you see them to eat?'

'Ah, cherry-berries are different, Chip *putha*. They have a kind of glow which you can only see when you get to my age: senile and dodo-headed. You see these fruity-booties snook in the summery sun into a huge and mighty heap and then they doodles it out bit by bit.' Her slowly blinding eyes would twinkle, 'Bite by bite.' She would suck and shape each word in her mouth like a child with a sweet.

Sometimes she would ask if I had any news of *home*. The old town. She would only ask about the place, the politics, the economy. 'What's the crooning, Chip *putha*?' Although she never mentioned Prins I could sense her body stiffen underneath the folds of matured fat – a new alertness – when I had news of him. When I came back from visiting him in 1991 I wanted to tell her how he was moving into new businesses, like his father Jason; learning the art of

making money from paintings, tourism out of terrorism. I
would hint of his successes to her although I never mentioned his emotional engagements. But if I spoke too much
about him, or things to do with him, she would steer the
conversation into areas where he was absent, as though his
final geographical rejection of her was too painful for her to
bridge.

'You know, when first I came to this daffodil country it
was very different.' She held her throat and repeated the
phrase in an absurdly plummy accent. '*Such* a different
country.'

'You mean different from home.'

'No, Chip *putha*. Different from now.'

I pictured streets without cafés, buildings before sand-
blasting, rooms with no central heating.

'We had buckets of *time* in those days.' Her lips met in a
tight curved line. 'Time to care.' She said it as though she
somehow knew that she no longer had time, that suddenly
time was no longer on her side. She had memory but no
time. It made no sense to me then. Only now am I beginning to understand how time might run out. Will run out
for all of us.

III

LATE MORNING

'You know, I can't eat this stuff back home. I just wallop it down here but it's impossible to eat it at home.' Prins was talking about the muesli I had given him as if it was still in front of him; it had already disappeared. 'Must be the heat. You know, you feel it coming like a wave even early in the morning there.'

'Have some more?' I nudged the sack of cereal closer to him with my elbow, the way Pearl used to do with me.

'Or maybe it's the milk. Do you think it's just the milk that makes the difference?' He pushed the bowl away from him. 'Or maybe I just can't face it with the stuff that's going on at home. Even breakfast cereal is in the hands of bloody killers now, you know?' I thought Prins was talking to banish silence and the spectres of the past. I couldn't help wondering how Pearl would have reacted if he had come a few days earlier. Perhaps I should have called him myself and not lived in that idle mixture of hope and inertia. It all works out, I used to think, it all works out in the end. My faith in time used to be absolute: a universal rhythm making a pattern to our days. But then death, or departure, breaks the pattern. Fakes a new pattern, and we are none the wiser.

'You want a bath or something? Rest?'

Prins stretched back. 'No, I must get some clothes, *men*. But where is Naomi? Where d'you think she is?'

I asked him whether he had the right number.

'What d'you mean?'

'She has her own place now, you know.'

He grunted as if he had momentarily forgotten, but he knew nothing about it.

I tried the right number, but there still was no answer. 'Maybe she's at the old flat with the dead phone.' Prins cocked his head to one side. 'Have you seen her recently?'

'Naomi?'

'Yes, *men*, Naomi. D'you know what's going on?'

'She's coping,' I said. 'It's a heavy time, you know, in her condition. She's enormous,' I made a globe out of my arms. 'Like a huge balloon.'

'Little Naomi?'

I nodded. 'You know she is pregnant?'

'Nobody told me.'

'Nobody tells you anything, do they?' I laughed, but I felt guilty.

He laughed too. 'I guess I have my secrets, and they have theirs.'

I had always thought of Prins as someone who put all his cards on the table. He seemed to be one of those people who wants to share his whole life and all his thoughts with his friends. He would discuss his plans with everyone. He carried his world in his head and had a way of making it immediately accessible to those around him. I was his audience and his sidekick.

Prins was always doing things: getting jobs, quitting jobs. I could hardly keep track. He used to love talking about them. Within minutes I would feel that I knew the people he knew just as well as he did. His colleagues became my colleagues; his adversaries my adversaries. Their characteristics, their personalities, their peculiarities – as seen by Prins – became instantly familiar. But then he moved on, leaving me behind with a bunch of dinosaurs I had nothing in common with except Prins himself. Or, by then, his shadow. His fast-lane life vicariously became mine; his loves my unquenchable crushes; his abandoned dreams, my enduring ones. That was always the way it seemed, but perhaps he kept some things back, like the rest of us. Some deeper, darker secrets. Or maybe he had changed once he went back to an older island.

'Secrets?' I echoed.

He shook his head smugly. 'So, *chuti* Naomi is havings *ze* baby, and I am going to be *ze grand-oncle*. My God, are we so *ancien*? How did all this happen?'

'She met a guy called Dylan,' I said.

o

I was at Pearl's place the day Naomi, her only grandchild and the one who lived with her for almost all of the last ten years of her life, first came back with news of Dylan. She had met him at the video shop down the road where she had gone to return one of Pearl's all-time classics: *High Noon*.

'He sort of glows a bit,' she said.

'What? Is he a light bulb?' Pearl cut in.

'He just gets very red,' Naomi couldn't stop smiling. 'But he is so *sweet*. We're going to the Odeon on Friday.'

'So, he's a sugar almond that glows in the dark?'

Naomi laughed happily, ignoring the gibe, and described Dylan to both of us. 'He is a little chubby but he has lovely rich brown hair, wonderful eyes and a really cute tiny gold earring like a fish.'

'A goldfish in his ear?' Pearl pulled at her own smooth lobe doubtfully.

'He likes *High Noon*,' Naomi challenged Pearl. 'And he can whistle the theme tune beautifully.'

Pearl was speechless for a moment, disarmed by the vision of a slightly chubby, Technicolor Gary Cooper strolling out of the flutter of a film-frame into her sunset sitting room, thrumming her heart softly with her favourite tune: 'Do Not Forsake Me . . .'

o

After Naomi started frequenting the cinema with Dylan, I suggested to Pearl that she too might enjoy a visit. The local Odeon had been refurbished but still retained the faded aura of an old-fashioned temple of fantasy, a mid-century mustiness trapped by loops of unspooled celluloid.

'No fear,' she refused and pulled out her knitting needles. 'How can I go? I need my sofa and a bit of knitting to get through the dull bits, you know. I'm not like our Dylan.'

'What do you mean, not like Dylan?'

'You see, that boy is too modern. He can't sit still unless he is forced to. If he watches a video he says he can't stop that fast-forwarding business for the boring parts. Nimsi says, only in the cinema he sits still. Mind you, that's the last place I'd have thought he should be sitting still with a pretty girl like her next to him. But you see, I don't need to go *out* to sit still, no? I can see the whole picture nicely right here, thank you.'

○

I didn't think Naomi and Dylan would last beyond a few months. I was happy for her. I could see how his fingers might have reached into her heart, plugging each valve and ventricle until it seemed almost to burst in a big red corpuscular corona, but I was sceptical about his long-term intentions. Perhaps it was because of the fragrance of jasmine oil I noticed when we first met, and his Phuket resort T-shirt.

But then Naomi came back one day and told Pearl that Dylan had proposed to her. '*Yes!*' Pearl yelled and clapped her hands. Her knitting wool bounced all over the room. But Naomi seemed affronted by the idea. 'I'm not sure I'm ready . . .'

'What, child? What's the problem with you? If you are going to make a life with him, you better get on with it. There aren't too many years in a life, you know.'

'How many is too many?' Naomi wanted to know.

'You'll know,' Pearl said. 'You'll find out.'

'I like him,' Naomi protested. 'I really like him.'

'Don't tell us, darling,' Pearl's eyes widened. 'Tell him. How many years you want to keep him hanging on?'

'Trouble is, I don't want to get married, you know. And he is so conservative really, deep down inside that's all he wants.'

'And what the zooks do you want, Nimsi child?'

Naomi rubbed her ear. 'I can't tell you . . . yet.'

o

When I recounted Naomi and Dylan's early courtship, Prins looked forlorn. 'I'd forgotten how easy it was to fall in love here. I wonder what *Amma* would have said if she'd been in Colombo these last few years.'

'Why?'

'Lola. You know? She is a Vatunas.'

I knew Lola. During my visit in 1991 Prins had talked enough about her. 'She used to live next door. When I was a kid we never played with anyone next door, but I do have a vague recollection of a girl in a *dot-dot* frock. How was I to know it was the same girl when we met her that time in Birkenhead, years ago. Remember? She remembers you. She was an art student then. Ten – actually thirteen – years later, she's become a real artist.'

I never told Pearl about Lola. I just never did. I didn't think that relationship would come to anything either, at the time. Not with the Lola I had remembered.

○

Three months after Dylan's rejected proposal Naomi discovered she was pregnant.

Dylan found Naomi too moody to talk to him. She didn't want any other intrusion in her life. There was enough coming at her from the inside. In desperation Dylan came to Pearl.

He had stood in front of Pearl like a schoolboy. His curly hair brushed down carefully. His shoes shining. Pearl, recounting his visit to me later, took two sharp breaths, 'I could smell the polish, you know. Boy, were those shoes gleaming.'

Naomi had gone to Mothercare: an afternoon's outing. Pearl made the tea, slowly, and then searched around the larder for her tin of biscuits. It was Dylan who had found it on the bottom shelf.

'I told him to bring it in with the tea,' she explained to me. Dylan had fixed her lopsided trolley while he was there; he has the knack for that sort of practicality.

'I asked him to have a ginger nut. He had it. Tougher than concrete, you know. I wish I could eat them but these teeth they give now wouldn't last a minute. But that girl Nimsi, my goodness, she crunches through them at a rate. Loves ginger. So this boy Dylan then tells me that she won't even speak to him now. With his baby she is too. I told him, not to worry. It had all happened a bit suddenly and with babies, you can never tell how people will react, you know. But I always say, it is a rare thing for life to happen to plan tak-tak-tak like that. Sometimes it gets a little unpredictable. That is us, after all. Isn't that so? We'd be dead before we knew it if everything just went according to plan, no?'

Pearl had done her best to reassure him, '"Give her time," I told him. "Give her time." That's all we need. Whether we are young or old, all we need is a little time.'

'What do your parents think about all this?' she had asked. All she had known of them was that they lived in Wales with a view of the sea.

Dylan had shrugged. 'I don't know. It's not something we've talked about.' He too was one for not telling. Being silent until it is too late.

'Whatever happens they will understand,' Pearl had said.

She had asked Dylan how often he went to see them. 'Christmas, birthdays, sometimes in the spring or the summer – Barmouth is a bit of a journey,' he had replied, neatly deflating the memory of his last quarrel with his father about direction – the lack of it – that had been bubbling up.

'The air must be good,' Pearl paused and looked at me. 'Seagulls and all?' I contemplated the empty grey sky outside.

Since the death of her first child, Pearl had hardly moved out of her patch of London, less than a square mile around Almeida Avenue, except to the cemetery to bury the next of her children. But in the years before that, she felt, she had travelled enough in the world to see that it did not change much from place to place; not as much as it changed with the passing of time. 'It's time that wreaks havoc with us, you know. Plays hell with everything.' But to Dylan she had simply said, 'Give our Nimsi time. For now, time will heal.'

O

All summer she had been trying to wean Naomi away from her. But towards the end of August Pearl had fallen in her bedroom and hurt her wrist. Naomi felt she ought to stay and look after her.

'Nimsi darling, at this stage in my life all I need is my energy to keep body and soul together, you know.' The flesh on her arm rippled as she lifted her hands in exasperation.

Soft, brown, creamy flesh loosening on her old, old bones. 'What I need is stillness. Things to settle down. You must go to him. Staying here in your state helps nobody. Not for me, don't stay.'

But each time I saw her Naomi looked more and more sullen.

'You should be happy,' Pearl scolded her. 'What is this nonsense?'

Naomi sat down on a dining chair and patted the side of her belly gently.

'Look at you,' Pearl moved her head from side to side, 'there's a four-month-old baba in there, kicking up your tummy, and no father even to feel it move. What's the meaning of that?' Pearl turned to me. 'What do *you* say?'

I said I thought babies don't have to have their fathers casting shadows over their lives; not even their mothers. Like Naomi, I never knew mine. We all just need someone to call our own; to name rather than to be named by.

Naomi looked gratefully at me.

'Is that so?' Pearl stared at me as though I was completely off my head. 'If they can't, all right. I can understand that. I also have had to go through it all. But when you have the father there, then what is the problem?'

'It's complicated, Gran. So complicated.'

'What is this complication? You two made the baby, so what is now the complication?'

Naomi did not seem to want to say anything about the practical difficulties. I told Pearl that the problem was that Naomi did not want to leave Pearl. She wanted Dylan to come and stay with her at Almeida Avenue, but he was too embarrassed.

'Don't be so silly. If the silly girl wants him to stay here, why can't he? What is there to be embarrassed about? The baby is there, no? Proof of the pudding and all that. Does he not want to be with her?'

'It's not that, Gran.'

Dylan was always hatching plans for them to be together, but these did not include moving into number 52b Almeida Avenue with Naomi's nearly octogenarian grandmother. At first they had been about fresh starts, sex outside bedrooms, love scents in his antique bathtub and butter off their own dining table; but since the pregnancy was confirmed he drew plans of sunlit nursery rooms and meadow-land playpens to entice her.

It was only when Pearl began to complain that Naomi and her pregnancy were beginning to drain the energy out of her that Naomi started to feel she had better move out.

When I went over on Bonfire Night with my traditional packet of sparklers, Naomi pushed me into the kitchen. 'What shall I do?' she whispered. 'She talks of feeling drained, just like Ravi did.'

'Maybe it's another one of those anniversaries: her mother's, or father's, or your mother's, or Jason's, or maybe she's just frustrated that she can't knit so much after that wrist problem . . .'

'No, it's to do with me.'

I told her I couldn't tell her what to do. Nobody could. But Pearl had been more forthright. 'Get going, girl,' she had chided her. 'Get out of here before it's too late.'

After about ten days of Naomi's anxious nail biting and hair washing at Almeida Avenue, I got a telephone call from Pearl.

'She's gone,' Pearl sighed. 'At last she has gone to him.'

I asked whether she – Pearl – was all right.

'I am fine. Very good. Such a relief, that girl going at last.'

The autumn trees outside were stripped bare as though their inner, secret convulsions had to be revealed like twisted fingers to the world; the pavement was completely hidden by dead leaves – gold flakes. I could appreciate the need for her to see Naomi more settled, but I was worried about how Pearl would manage on her own. Would my visits to her now turn into a necessary chore rather than occasions for exploration? I didn't want to become her helpline, her support system, although she had become mine.

'Don't worry,' she said. 'I can see all I need to see. Dylan's arranged a home help. And, at last, I have my own place. When you need to wind down, you need to do it at your own speed, Chip *putha*, on your own.'

ဂ

'But she would have liked to have seen the baby, her first great-grandchild, wouldn't she?' Prins looked unsure, as he struggled to take in all the news I had given him.

Pearl was very proud of the pregnancy, I told him, even though Naomi wasn't married to Dylan. It had changed all of their lives.

'You'd think she'd have hung on then. Don't people pull through until something crucial happens – like a birth.'

Pearl *had* hung on until Wednesday, when the baby was due. But it hadn't come. 'She would have waited to see you too, but she couldn't. There wasn't time even to ask for you.'

'I would have come earlier, if I'd known this was going to happen.' Prins hesitated. He scraped his thumbnail against his front tooth. 'I wanted to talk to her. There's a lot to clear up, you know.'

'It was more sudden than planned,' I said, 'although perhaps she knew what was coming.' Maybe we all do. Don't people always know about their final end? I regretted never even writing to Prins before that, not marking the passage of time with a few lines about our lives. I had not thought it important until that day when, suddenly, I began to see the gulf that lay between us. How the connections between all of us could disappear forever. Looking back, I wish I had said more to Prins about the Pearl I had grown to know in his absence.

Prins got up from his chair and began to pace the floor, peering out of the window at the damp grey wall that overshadowed my back garden. The sound of a dustbin being dragged across concrete made him wince.

'Let's go. I really need some new clothes,' he announced finally. 'Where can we try?'

'You want a suit or what?'

'How's about a leather tanga? Anything goes now, isn't that what they say? Motherless, fatherless, Godless, knickerless.' Prins laughed and then stretched out his arms. For what could have been one nanosecond he looked lost, and much older. 'I need some jeans. Black jeans. And maybe a jumper or something. Let's go. What d'you say?'

o

The light outside was deceptively bright. A patch of sky had cleared. Prins buttoned up the sheepskin coat I had lent him and looked around, surprised. 'What happened?' he asked.

'The sun comes, even here,' I said.

The winter sun had turned all the windows of the Victorian terrace opposite into reflective rectangular pools. At the shop by the clock tower Prins bought his clothes, humming to the riffs of Suede escalating out of enormous black boxes stacked with garments.

'OK?' a ginger-haired boy enquired.

Prins shook a leg. 'A bit narrow, but it feels great. Just great.' He sounded like he did years ago when it was all FUs and high spirits. Things were different now, but I could see he was thinking of those days, before all our troubles became so overwhelming.

That was when Mira, Prins and I saw each other all the time and never reciprocated anything in the right direction. Mira was in love with Prins, and I with her. Prins was in love with his dreams. Sometimes Mira's friend Tripti, another of her eager *amorettos*, fresh from Singapore, joined us. She often came with a retinue of her own. Students from around the world – Malaysia, India, Indonesia – who sipped Kardomah coffee and watched people like Mira and Prins crack open the city any way they wanted to. We were the *visa people*. Temporary residents: time-bound, would-be immigrants of the 1970s. Permanently temporary except for Prins; he was the only one with the right to reside, a

Mastercard, and a home in London. A creditworthy honorary member. And he was the first to leave Britain for dreamland.

On the way back from the shops Prins grew serious again and asked if he could telephone Colombo before it got too late. 'I don't have a lot of time.'

'Can't you stay just a few days more?'

'It's impossible. I have to be back for Monday. It could change everything for me. And I had to get this special ticket: two transfers, airports in God-knows-where, hellish flights. But there was no other way. Anyway, there's nothing here for me now.'

'What about Naomi?'

'She has her life,' he sighed. 'But I wish my mother had told me more.'

'Did she write?' I asked.

He turned and looked straight at me and shook his head. 'No,' he said, but in a way that made me feel he was not being entirely truthful. The clock in the clock tower behind us stuttered. The midday winter sun spun paler than before, beginning to vanish behind a thickening snow cloud. I sensed something odd in the fast-freezing air between us. 'No, she never said anything that helped. But . . .' he turned away without saying any more. He walked slowly, gauging his thoughts, choosing his words.

After a while he broke the silence. 'I wrote to *Amma*

recently. I asked her some things.' He spoke softly as if he was speaking to himself. 'You know, my father died in 1956. They say it was an accident. But, I don't know, I am beginning to think there was more to it than that.'

IV

NOON

When we got back to my house, I told Prins to use the phone in the study.

'I'll get the cost from the operator afterwards.'

'No, don't worry,' I said.

'I must pay,' he insisted. 'This will be a long conversation.' He took a deep breath, 'I'll try Naomi again as well, and the flat in case she's gone there.'

The flat at Almeida Avenue was in a large detached three-storey Victorian house. Pearl had the ground floor.

When I arrived to stay with her, Ravi, her younger son, had just come back from a year in America.

'What do you think, Chip *putha*, this is the boy who goes to America and loses his tinkerbell tongue.' Pearl would sigh and cluck in front of him. 'I thought people go to America to find something. *This one* seems to have lost it all.'

NOON

I only knew Prins after I first met Ravi; they were completely different from each other. Not only was Ravi quiet and uncommunicative but he had that learned air about him that made you feel a fool even before you opened your mouth. And he knew things about America which I could only imagine.

If Prins had been there instead of Ravi that first year I stayed at Almeida Avenue, I would never have got to know Pearl the way I did. Prins would have done all the talking. He turned up for a night at home three times in the nine months I was living there. Each time I would have to vacate his room and sleep on Pearl's sofa, but I didn't mind. He was instantly likeable despite the bursts of irritation he directed at his family. He seemed to trust strangers immediately as friends, and would fill the flat with his news. But in his absence it was Pearl who filled the void with words for me. She fed me stories, just as she fed me heart-stopping fried breakfasts and enormous buttery dinners. We didn't always all eat together. Sometimes Ravi would eat with us, sometimes we would take it in turns. In the evening the TV was always on and Ravi's silence would be lost in the sound of light entertainment. Every week Pearl would make rice and liver curry, cottage pie and macaroni cheese in strict rotation. She had become quite round by then, and with each meal I could feel all of us getting a little bit fatter. She used butter for everything. Pearl insisted that the best thing in England was the quality of the milk and therefore the butter. 'It's the grass,' she'd say. 'There's no grass like this anywhere else in the world. To be a cow here must be to be in heaven.' In a way it is as well that she didn't live longer to discover what would eventually happen to the cows in England.

A few months before I had to move out of Almeida Avenue, because of Prins's homecoming at the end of his stint up north, I discovered it was Ravi's twenty-third birthday. The first I knew of it was when Pearl shuffled into the sitting room carrying a lopsided chocolate cake on a breadboard. Two table candles burned perilously together, jammed into the centre of the cake. 'Happy Birthday!' she hollered and Ravi eventually emerged from his room. I made the tea and we celebrated in silence with the TV off and the wax dripping onto the sugar icing.

Pearl told me he had not wanted a party. He had said he had no friends. 'Not like Prins, you know,' Pearl pulled in her lips, steadying her face. 'If he was here, it would be pandemonium.' But Prins didn't even call. Ravi seemed relieved. He was never pleased to hear the telephone ring.

After we had finished tea I went out and bought two bottles of Spanish wine. I was determined to make a party out of the evening.

That was one night we did all eat together. Pearl had cooked biriani to celebrate. Each mouthful seemed to have a pound of clarified butter in it. '*Ghee*,' Ravi said in his rarely used transatlantic accent. After we had eaten, Ravi, curiously groggy, stayed at the table with me; we still had another bottle of red wine to finish. When Pearl went to bed, I filled the fluted plastic tumblers to the brim.

I said I wanted to know about America, and he slowly told me about his trip. It was as if the biriani had greased his mouth and the wine finally loosened his tongue.

○

Ravi pointed at the bookshelves in the sitting room. 'I first discovered America in poetry. She, my mother, of course thinks America is just Hollywood. For Prins it is a Mecca of cars and cowboys. But for me it was an enormous poem: *Hiawatha*, *Song of Myself*, *Howl*. I wanted to hear it and see it, *be* there. *Find* it. Discover it like the Inuit, or Alastair Cook. I thought that it would be where I would want to live forever. I had an idea like those immigrants in the films my mother watches all day, setting off from Sicily for New York. The New World. Except for me it was almost an *old* world I was looking for. A place I would recognize and feel I had arrived. Perhaps even come across myself already living there. Find my footsteps and think, this is where that sound I heard came from. That was what I believed.'

That was how Pearl came to England. In love with a shadow in her head that she couldn't quite focus on until she got here. Perhaps Ravi was simply repeating her own journey to England, but with different co-ordinates.

'I spent almost an entire year in America,' Ravi dipped his head into the tumbler of red wine. 'And at the end of it, I turned around and came back.' He said it as if he was describing a walk to the corner shop. As if he had bought a packet of cigarettes, or a can of beer, and returned.

'So now you know,' I said. 'You know America.'

Ravi poured himself more wine. 'These tumblers belong in Sidcup,' he frowned. 'For dentures, not wine.'

He had an older face than Prins, even though he was the younger of the two. Some discolouration of his skin made dark patches under his eyes and on one side of his mouth. He always looked weary.

'In America everybody wants too much,' he said. 'I found it extraordinary: this wanting. And although they seemed so different from what I had expected, they were not unlike me. No one seemed to know why they were there: I mean in that precise place. They could have been anywhere. Everybody I saw in that small town, on the out-skirts of the outskirts of Washington, was looking for some idea of some place they thought was America. Sometimes you felt rather drained by it. As though everyone was taking something out of you. Your idea of yourself. Everybody seemed to be looking for something; and yet you had this vast sense that it was all for nothing.'

Ravi frowned again and rubbed the middle of his fore-head with two of his fingers. He rubbed it like a prayer. Some esoteric American mystic ritual. Or maybe it was just a family trait. I could hear the soft skin of his fingers taking the sheen off his forehead, darkening it like a clot of blood.

'At first they thought I was English. An *Englishman*.' A bubble of laughter burst out of his loosened lips. He rubbed his forehead harder. 'They could hear it in the accent on the telephone. My brownskin face was a bit of a shock. I was *told* this. It was extraordinary.' He almost choked on the memory wriggling under his fingers. 'In this country, it is my skin that people notice, that goes in front of me, every-where. People look at me and they see darkness first. Even my shadow seems darker to them than theirs. Everything else follows to fit. But if you have no flesh to hook your foolishness to, I suppose you make a body out of an accent.' He blew out the rest of a lungful of heavy air as if he had been holding it in his chest for months. 'They are easy people to say hello to, but I was feeling very drained, you know. You feel as though something is disappearing out of you all the time.' He blew some more air out, like a swimmer.

o

The day before Prins came back to reclaim his room, I moved out to a small studio flat I had found a short bus ride away. I was sad to leave what had become my haven, but I could see that Pearl was both excited and nervous about the return of her Prins. After I had packed my cases and carried them into the hall, she went into the room and turned the bed around. 'I want him to feel he has come back to the same room,' she explained, '*his* room.' She put out some fresh linen I had not noticed before. But before I finally left the flat she made me promise to come back for a meal with Prins the next day. 'And every day, if you like. You are also my *putha* now, no?'

When I saw Prins the next day he was insistent, 'Chip, have you been to Greenwich? I'll take you there tomorrow, and then we can go to this amazing Thai restaurant Mira has discovered by the river.' Although I had been living in London for months, Prins was the one who introduced me to the wider surroundings of the world I eventually made my own.

o

Unlike Prins, and unlike me, Ravi never moved out of Pearl's flat. After his return from America he got a job as a payroll clerk in the town hall and settled into a routine that seemed to meet his needs without upsetting his dreams. He kept no letters, no diaries, no evidence of his thoughts. Besides a few American poetry books, and the *Norton* anthology, his only other quirk was to collect used tickets: bus tickets, train tickets, proof of any journey – testaments of the regular, necessary outings to his office – the coupon of his flight to New York, the counterfoil of a voucher to Washington and back. All of these were carefully ordered by month and year in a blue Lever-arch file. The file was right up to date. It was kept on his small desk along with an old, portable manual typewriter which seemed permanently encased. He also had a tumbler with a picture of black and white highland terriers and a whisky slogan printed on it on the desk. This was filled with paper clips.

Occasionally, in the early years after I moved out, he

would disappear for a night or two. He never said where he was going. Pearl always hoped he was going to see someone special: a girl, but neither she nor I ever met any friend of his. He would time his excursions for when Mira, Tripti and I came for feeding. But if we surprised him and he was already stuck inside, he would try to slip into his room and lock the door. Mira called him La Trappe, the silent professor.

'Why does he never like to bring anyone home, nobody to this flat? Not like Prins, or even you. Never. He likes everything to be in its place. After that trip to America, it's as if there is nothing else to do. He puts everything in order and that's it.' Pearl could not understand how he could have gone to America and then become so cloistered. 'I thought he would be bursting with vitality and want to see the whole world. We are a migratory people, you know, but this one won't even move an inch now.' She never considered that Ravi's foray into America constituted the journey of a lifetime. And that, unlike Prins, he had decided once was enough. There was nowhere else to go, and no means of escape from the present.

Year by year Ravi became ever more reclusive. In the end he refused to go out of the house at all except to his office and to do very basic chores: shopping early on Saturday morning, the bank on Monday, putting the rubbish out on Thursday. But Pearl found the sound of his breath comforting. What she wanted from him was different from what she wished for from Prins. For her, Ravi seemed to be always there, filling the empty space in the flat, while the rest of us drifted in and out as we pleased.

Prins found their lives insufferable. 'What the hell's the point in hiding here?' Prins would point at his huddled mother with one hand and Ravi's impenetrable door with the other. 'Who could live in a madhouse like this?' he would explode. Pearl ignored his outbursts. 'Prins has yet to grow,' she would confide in me whenever he stormed out of the flat. 'He has a lot of catching up to do, you know.'

Prins sailed in and out of the flat all the time. Often he would go away for weeks on end, chasing some dream of a life he wanted, while Ravi remained the anchor. But perhaps each in his own manner was finding a way of moving out of reach. Pearl indulged them both, even though neither of her two sons seemed to indulge her. She acted as though she didn't mind, until it was too late; then it seemed there was nothing anyone could do in recompense.

o

Prins was quite solemn when he came out of my study. He didn't say anything about his call to Colombo, although later I found a twenty-pound note under the receiver. He only said that he still could not get through to Naomi. 'Let's go to the flat, anyway.'

Cars had encroached on the narrow tarred pavement outside the front gate. We squeezed past a line of Citroëns, Pandas, Audis and a Nissan with a smashed quarter window. Crumbled glass sparkled like a Shangri-La night under our feet.

'You have a car?' Prins asked.

'Yes,' I said. 'An old car. It's down the other street. Space wars, you know.'

'At least it's not like our bloody war: the people's war,' Prins grunted. 'Sinhala kids, Tamil kids, it's all the same. Fodder for the politicos. On every side the rich are scheming and the rest are reeling.'

I shrugged and led him down past a derelict Ford. I wouldn't know what was going on anywhere at the best of times.

The bare cherry trees along the road prodded the wintry sky, swelling it. Prins walked with his head tilted up. 'In April, these will turn the whole street pink,' I explained, forgetting that he had lived in the area for nearly as long as I had.

Pearl loved pink flowers. Whenever I brought her a bunch of pinks, her eyes would light up. She would put the flowers in a glass vase on top of the television and watch them until the heads drooped and the water turned green.

○

When Pearl lived in Arcadia she had a gardener: Sunderam. Pearl knew nothing about gardening but she got Sunderam to plant every kind of flower she could name: some would bloom just once, others would struggle through for two seasons. She and Sunderam never perfected the art but she lived in hope.

In London, her flat overlooked a garden which belonged to somebody else. There was no Sunderam to control it or to renew it. A dogwood shrub dominated one side. On the other side, in front of the kitchen window, a plum tree would blossom in spring madness. Blossom time was a good time for Pearl: she would fling open her grey windows and declare, 'Spring has *sprung*.' But in recent years spring arrived later and later for her. The blossom would come but the windows would open only a little. Then close soon after. It was too cold. 'It gets *very* cold very suddenly in this country,' she would mutter and shut the window. Sometimes the electric fire would be on while the sun blazed outside.

'You remember the blossom trees?' I asked Prins.

He nodded. 'The plum in the garden? The bloody mess below afterwards when the wind blew.'

o

We parked under one of the bitter-cherry trees outside the house. By this time clouds had blotted most of the day's weakening light. The grey steps to the front door sagged as if the earth was hollow below the path.

'I really don't think anyone is here,' I said.

'Where the hell is everybody then?'

I said that there was no *everybody*. There was only Naomi now and she didn't live in the flat any more. Prins snorted. He rang the bell and knocked loudly on the front door. The curtains were not drawn but there was no sign of life in the darkness inside. The nets hung in grey streaks like a winter's dawn. I had not looked at the place in this way before. Someone had started to repair the gutters.

'You know the bastard landlords never wanted to do anything when she was in here. Even when I lived here.' Prins stepped back and scanned the front of the house. 'And look, now she's gone, in two minutes they are sprucing it up, even in this bloody cold.'

Noon

I asked Prins whether he wanted to look around the outside. There was a side door that led to the back garden and the outside stairs. He shrugged, 'Why not?'

The path was of yellow gravel the colour of sand and the consistency of a nut crunch. A quince grew on one wall of the house. The door itself was painted colonial green and it opened onto a garden that looked as wild as ever, even in the winter. Brambles sprawled under the yellow dogwood bursting at the back, but the plum tree was as bare as the arms of Venus. In a corner the brown twigs of a forsythia sprang out in a quiver of frozen arrows. Near the steps, going up to a terrace added onto the old house, someone had started to make a flower bed. The black earth had been scooped up to reveal the clay underneath. But it seemed as though the winter had overtaken the best of intentions. One or two blades of a crocus had sprouted in the false spring, and a bedraggled lavender bush meandered around a pile of rusty tins and rocks that had been chucked together into a Dadaist rockery. I saw a startled blackbird hopping about under a mutilated tea rose. Every twig seemed to have a patina of ice, or impending ice. The air itself was hard with the expectation of snow.

Prins surveyed the little plot silently.

'Has it changed?' I asked.

He shrugged again. 'I can't tell. I don't really remember

any more.' He turned away and headed back towards the car. 'Let's go,' he said. 'We'll have to get the keys from Naomi and come back. There must be a helluva lot to do in there and I've only got tomorrow.'

'There's also a couple of things to settle about the funeral,' I told him, 'after you see Naomi.'

'With the undertakers?'

'Well, more the service . . . the rest has been taken care of.' I didn't think he was ready to handle the undertakers yet. There would be time for that the next day, after he had got used to being back in a place where neither he nor Pearl lived any more.

o

As we couldn't find Naomi, I took Prins out for lunch to Mister Moon's. It was crowded with local students and out-of-work actors, but we managed to find a table by a misted window. I cleared the condensation with a serviette. I could only see the side of the old church from where I sat; Prins could see the whole road leading down to the high street. Traffic lights blinked. A flower shop bloomed on the corner.

'Do you remember anything from when you were five or

six years old? That age or earlier?' Prins asked, surfacing from the silence he had slipped into in the car.

'A few things,' I replied.

'Strange,' he said. 'I can remember so little. It's all so murky.'

'The brightest years, surely?'

'Yes, but you see it was when my father died. I guess I've blocked a lot of it out.'

Then he told me that recently he had been trying to find out what had really happened back in 1956. 'Trouble is, when I look back I see him and everything else through so many filters. Nothing you can be sure of, you know. It makes it all very difficult. I have to build it up, pixel by pixel, in my mind.'

'What about the house?' I asked. Arcadia. 'Do you remember it?'

'I can't tell,' he said. 'Sometimes it's there like a dream, but I don't know whether what I remember comes from what I imagine now or from a real memory. D'you know the feeling?'

Maria, the café owner's daughter, came to take our order. Prins went for a Mister Moon's special: nasi goreng with prawns; I asked for a pepper salad and beer for both of us.

'And your mother? What about your mother?' Pearl was the one who had just died after all. Jason had died long ago and, it seemed to me, in a different world altogether.

Prins stared down. 'I am not sure I understand my own feelings. I have been thinking about her and him. How it could have turned out so differently if he had lived. For a long time I've cut out, you know. Blown and flown. I was trying to understand something about *him* first. And she always seemed to me to be somehow in the way, you know, like a screen. I felt I had to get at it all in another way, from another direction.' He sighed. 'Then, recently I began to see it was totally impossible. I was sort of making my way back when . . .' he closed his eyes for a moment.

'But there is one memory,' he bit the tip of his tongue very gently as it peeped out of his mouth. 'I had forgotten, but there is one thing, you know. A really strong memory from deep down under. I can see it now, in front of me, as if I am there.

'I must have been about five. I was in the garden. Our garden, I suppose. But it was a big garden. And it had coconut trees. Can that be? Coconut trees?' He squinted. 'I've been to see the house we lived in then – Arcadia. I don't know where the coconut trees could have been. It doesn't fit, but I remember sitting against a coconut tree, sort of against the beard. You know, at the bottom of the trunk? I've got a toy in my hand, a toy gun. Can't quite make out whether it is small or big. Can't focus on it, you know. Sometimes it looks like one of those plastic things – a cowboy's Colt .45, and then sometimes it feels like just a small, heavy, metal model derringer. A cap-gun. The picture won't stay still.

'But I am there, playing. I have bluesey shorts on. No, wait. It's the *man* who has the bluesey shorts. I can't see his face. He is tall, not like my father. He is so tall I can't see his face. He goes up to the clouds. There is no sound. This is memory with no soundtrack. D'you know what I mean? But everything is tall. Coconut trees, a man in bluesey shorts, and something else behind that is tall and throwing a long shadow over everything. I can see weirdo colours, you know. Neon green, from the grass I guess, and the fuzzy grey from the tree trunk. That's clear. And the bluesey shorts. And then this shadow that kind of gooks everything and makes it dark. Then it gets dimmer and dimmer and disappears. But I feel guilty. Like I shouldn't remember. Some crushing sense of guilt. Not that I was doing anything. Not even playing with myself. I don't think that sense of guilt is in the boy there: me. But it somehow washes over it all. Like a film of water or something. Why guilt?' Prins tilts his head and looks at me but doesn't really want me to speak.

'And that grass. I don't comprehend that bloody grass. I can remember sitting there against the tree, on the grass. Comfortable. Yes, really comfortable. A toy gun in my hand. I am wearing shorts too. I can't tell the colour. Must be white. Baggy. Nothing else. But I am sitting comfortably on the grass. The softest grass. It makes no sense. You can't sit on the grass in any of those gardens now, can you? It's so thick and hard. It's like sitting on cactus now. But what I remember is like sea-side grass, you know. Or up-country grass. Soft. Blue. Spongy. I don't understand it.'

'Maybe you had grass like that then,' I suggested, wrapping a strand of roasted yellow pepper around my fork. 'Soft grass.'

'Grass for the arse,' Prins laughed. 'That's the way it was. Our whole history is just a squabble about whose arse is on whose grass.'

'So where's yours?' I asked. 'You still have the house in the hills? That garden?'

'Garden? You should see my garden now. In Colombo though, not in the hills. I've moved, you know. Always the mover. But the grass there is a real pain. Thirty square foot of ultimo agony. Fakir grass.'

O

'My father was forty-nine when he died. A hellava lot seems to have happened in the last eight years of his life.' Prins dabbed at his mouth with a serviette. 'It was the eight years in that house. Arcadia. Can you imagine? They move into this house and it becomes a mausoleum. I was born in a *mausoleum*. Maybe it should have been called that: Château Mausoleum.'

Prins began to count with his fingers. 'He went there when he was forty-one. You know what I did when I was forty-one?'

I shook my head.

'1991? You were there.'

Prins had been appointed General Manager of Gold Sands Enterprises – a group of hotels – and had moved into a company bungalow in the hills. Like father, like son: Prins too had become a real business visionary. He was brimming with pleasure. 'Look at this place,' he said to me when I visited him that year. 'Just take a head-blast look at it. Can you imagine a more fantastical setting anywhere in the world?' From his sitting room you could see the whole valley curdle with the misty milk of a mothering sky, coiling down around the uplands, feathering the whole world.

'That was the year I moved to our Shangri-La hotel. A few months later you came. At the same age, he and I, we both moved into the place of our dreams. What d'you make of that?'

Before I could say anything he carried on.

'My father had another eight years. I am quarter of the way through my eight now. Already I have moved back to bloody Colombo from Shangri-La.' His voice trembled

79

slightly, 'I want to know how much we are the same, but no one seems to know. Or wants to tell me.'

'It's just a coincidence,' I dismissed his maudlin thoughts. 'I mean, what about your father's father, for example. Did he also . . .'

'How can I know anything about his father when I know so little about *him*? All I know about the ancestors is what *Amma* used to say: we have a pinch of everyone in us, from the Veddah to the Scot, like most people.' His mouth dropped in a crooked line: a smile stepping down to an ineffable anxiety, an ulcer in his gut. 'But there is a possibility that I might move back into Arcadia. It belongs to Lola's family now.'

I started to ask about Lola, but Prins was not listening.

'You know something else,' he hissed. 'When *Amma* left home and came here, this bloody place, after he died, guess how old she was?'

I said nothing. A bus glided by on the road. An angel's whisper oiling its wheels.

'Forty-one.' His face tightened as he did a few more calculations in his head. 'When I'm forty-nine, *his* age when he died, it will be the last year of the century.'

'The end of the millennium.'

'That's it. The end of a lot of things.'

'So you reckon it's a century that belongs to you? Prins's century?'

His eyes twinkled. 'No, but maybe it will signify something. The Ducal century maybe, if we all die out. Hunted to extinction.'

'But there's Naomi,' I said, forgetting that she, his sister's daughter, doesn't carry the Ducal name.

'Yeah, there is Naomi . . .' Prins tossed back his head. 'Never mind. I was just thinking, that's all.'

o

Ravi's exit from the century of the Ducals came early, and was a carefully planned extinction. He withdrew slowly, without histrionics, until suddenly he was not there, more than a decade before *his* forty-first year.

Even Pearl found it a natural culmination of Ravi's peculiar ambition: to absent himself for longer and longer periods, until it became so long that one could not remember when he had left one's company and when he was due to come back.

He kept his job and did his chores right to the end, including the household shopping on the last day. He arranged everything. Ravi even organized his own funeral, the coffin, the cremation, the urn and its resting place in a newly constructed municipal vault in the cemetery. Even the inscription: 'I Don't Want to Set the World on Fire,' from an Ink Spots record he sometimes played while Pearl dozed in the afternoon. He had done his laundry on the last Saturday. There was nothing anybody else needed to do except mourn for a brief, regulated moment. The night he died, he was the one who made the telephone call to the doctor. By the time the doctor arrived Ravi was pulseless, dead on his carefully stripped bed. His shoes were polished and placed under his bed with a note to the doctor tucked into one, giving details of the lethal cocktail he had ingested. There was no other message.

About six months before Ravi died, Naomi had come to stay with Pearl. Prins had gone back to his dreamland by then, thoroughly fed up with his mother, his brother, the family and England. He had gone promising never to come back: an emigrating immigrant.

We all began to disperse: Tripti, Mira, and even me. I got into computers and had to relocate to Basingstoke for a few dreary months. But I kept coming back to London to visit Pearl whenever I could.

Ravi hardly acknowledged Prins's high-minded departure. He had stopped talking to the others years earlier, communicating only through shopping lists or telegraphic notes: 'Back soon' . . . 'Gone to bank' . . . 'Need butter'. Never signed, always anonymous. No evidence to positively link him to life. But when Naomi arrived to occupy Prins's room, he became more alert. It was as though he saw her as the one who would replace him in the Ducal household. It was impossible to tell who really held whom together with the Ducals. Both Ravi and Pearl could be seen as the backbone of a family which simply comprised the other; everybody else had disappeared.

Ravi was the one who had cleaned and rearranged Prins's room – the room I had stayed in once – for Naomi. He lined the drawers with scented paper and placed a small glass vase of yellow and purple freesias on a white linen handkerchief on the desk by the bed. He washed the curtains and cleaned the windows. He made sure the tiny wardrobe had its troop of metal hangers, a history of seasonal dry-cleaning, hanging in line with the twists of wire on the hooked stems screwing in the same uniform direction like a chorus on a secret Broadway.

Naomi was seventeen when she came. She had not wanted to study any more and had fallen out with her father over it. She hated school and felt she could no longer stay at home. She wanted to live in London and called her grandmother for help. Pearl told Naomi's father to give the girl time. You don't have to go to a fancy college to live a decent life. You have to make your life as you see it,' she reasoned down the telephone. Education had not helped Ravi, nor, as far as she could see, Prins. Anoja, Naomi's mother, never had the time for more than a short secretarial course.

In the end Naomi, like me, came to Pearl to find her feet. It seemed natural. We all need time.

She blossomed under the care of Ravi and Pearl. She told me later that at Almeida Avenue she felt she had entered the real world: shabbier, poorer, sadder than her father's modern, conventional Wilmslow home, but somehow truer to her inner sense. She learned to travel on the Underground and clean the tube dust out from under her nails with a Bic clip. She discovered a taste for Pearl's gut-roasting liver curry and ate butter with her rice. For the first three months she simply learned to live with a family that was not quite a family, among strangers who were not quite strangers. She would talk about growing up in Manchester, filling the old dark rooms of the flat with the sound of her seventeen unsung years. She was not interested in *their* past; it was their present and her past that were important to her.

Ravi began to sit in the sitting room with us, sipping whisky and listening, and not feeling any need to break the flow of chatter with his silence. 'He was head-to-toe content those last few months.' Pearl was baffled.

Pearl knew about death and dying. In her life so many people had passed away. First her elders, aunts and uncles, then her parents, then Jason, her friends, her first child. It was as though someone was plucking these lives from all around her like a fruit picker. When it came to Ravi, it was his own desire; he wanted no more. He had no will to go on. There was nothing else. Pearl turned out her small, plump hands, 'If he has no will, who can do anything?'

When I first saw her that painful summer after Ravi's suicide, she was quiet. She had the TV turned off. The news was too awful in every way. 'Why couldn't I give him the will to live?' Her face tightened, fighting back the tears. 'Why?'

○

Over the years Ravi seemed to have developed a plan to completely erase his life from the face of the earth. He not only tried not to make any impression in his daily life, but he tried to undo all past impressions. Sand down every surface he had touched so that there was no imprint left; wear away the shape of his image, and dull the daily perception of him until nothing remained to distinguish the figure from the background. Turn his solid flesh into something so transparent that it was barely there. He had been so meticulous over his exit that after he passed away not even a single letter arrived for him to remind anyone of his curtailed life. Not even the junk mail that daily disappoints the rest of us.

At his office he had attended to his final day of work as though it were the last rites of a true professional. There was apparently no unfinished business left on his desk. No unresolved cases. Nothing pending. No claims or disagreements to settle. Not even a scrap of extraneous information fluttering like a distress flag in the grille of an air vent. He had made it as easy as possible for his colleagues to forget him. He had never done anything unusual, except be meticulous. It was as if he knew no one ever remembers effortless efficiency, that over time other matters would fill the minds of all his colleagues and he would fade out of their consciousness. Their coffee-machine banter, the bitching at the photocopier, the deeper probing at the end of a winter's day between colleagues would bounce off other bodies until his name and prior existence would slip, like others before him, even out of the reach of history.

He had arranged for his death benefit to be paid directly into his mother's bank account. Pearl discovered that his modest Post Office savings had also been directed into it. There was no pension or further involvement necessary with his employers. Within three years all administrative traces of his existence in the office would have been destroyed and within seven years most other traces too. And in the foreseeable future, he would have known, there would be nothing of him remaining except the memories of those who were determined to remember him, or a few arbitrary images that flickered like flashes in the dark, a twitching worm of the imagination's fickle DNA. Even those would eventually give way to nothing. It was exactly as he would have wanted: a complete unravelling of an identity.

But he had not counted on Naomi and me, and on Prins coming back. He had not anticipated our needs. The hole that Pearl would leave. The hunger for history. The resilience of a story. Even one of disappearance.

O

Naomi was incensed.

'How could he do this?' she screamed. For her, Ravi, along with Pearl, and at a distance Prins, were the only known remnants of the mother she had never known. She was furious. She kept hammering on his door, as though he was asleep in his bed and needed to be woken up.

Pearl could not afford despair or to think of her own loss; it took all her powers to contain Naomi's ranting and railing. She tried to calm her and divine some sense out of Ravi's final abdication, but Naomi would have none of it.

'He didn't need to give up. What was the point? If nothing is so bloody important, why does he take the trouble to die? Why couldn't he just be here?' She shouted at Pearl and me as though we were Ravi's collaborators.

'I don't know, darling, I don't know,' Pearl cried. 'He wanted peace, I guess.'

'Peace is what he had,' sobbed Naomi. 'This *was* peace. There's no bloody peace when you're *dead*.'

o

In August the following year I moved to a dilapidated maisonette on Crescent Road, not far from Almeida Avenue. I began to travel more widely for my work, but there were lulls between assignments. Mira, Tripti and Prins having all gone their own way, I was lonely. I began to spend more time visiting Pearl, and Naomi if she happened to be in.

'It's like she's from another world,' Pearl would marvel whenever Naomi was out. 'Always going places.'

One evening, halfway through a bottle of sherry, Pearl told me about Naomi's mother. I knew very little of her. Like all of Pearl's brood she too seemed to have had the knack of leaving hardly a trace behind, except in the memories of those who survived her. 'Anoja was fourteen years older than Ravi and eleven years older than Prins, you know. Sometimes I can't believe it myself.' It meant that

Anoja was a surrogate mother to the two boys, especially Ravi, in the early years.

After Jason's death, Pearl had moved with all three children to her aunt's house up in the hills. In between nursing Ravi and settling the children and organizing their education – she hired private tutors because the schools were in as much disarray as herself – she travelled to and fro to sort out the estate and deal with Arcadia. She wanted to get rid of 'that carbuncle' as soon as she could. She sold it quickly. Land, she believed, had a propensity to fester. 'Rent, don't own, stay free,' was her maxim, even when she was eventually rooted to her Almeida Avenue flat in a country determined to make democracy permanently indebted to private ownership.

Anoja had been extraordinarily resilient about the changes in her world. Nothing seemed to affect her. 'Always such a strong girl,' Pearl would sigh as if still puzzled after all those years. But Anoja must have felt the gulf between her parents widen in the years they spent in Arcadia. Jason's death would have been a relief which she would have found distressing in itself. The escape from Arcadia would have brought such freedom that she must have felt she was breathing real air for the first time in her life only in her grandaunt's house in the hills, but it would also have cut her off from the wider world she was on the point of discovering.

She had been getting quite friendly with Baresh – the little sailor boy Pearl had mentioned before, now grown into quite a hulk – but her mother had not approved. He was related, however distantly. 'I never liked the idea of marrying in the family, you know. Sometimes I think that is the real trouble with *our* country: you find the same nose in every bed.' Pearl rocked over her knitting, speeding up her needles.

'But Anoja, unlike Prins, was never emotional anyway,' Pearl claimed. She always appeared to deal with crises matter-of-factly. It was a quality that Ravi, perhaps, learned from her. 'That child had the ability to quietly get on with whatever needed to be done, you know, without a fuss and without drawing attention all the time. Without being deflected.' Pearl spoke of Anoja more with respect than tenderness, as though this would expiate the guilt she felt at stifling her first romance and then abandoning her after Jason's death. 'But I was alone too, you know, when my mother died, and my father,' she would sometimes say as if to balance their lives. Or later, 'Maybe it is because I made her a mother to the boys that she couldn't live to be one, really, herself; and that has made me mother to Naomi.'

When Anoja came to England to be with Pearl, she was nineteen and by then determined to shape her life to her own needs. 'She wanted to be completely self-sufficient, you know. I suppose she watched the *pul* parts of my life and decided entanglements only brought confusion and misery.' Anoja had told her mother that she intended to work in an office and never get married.

'"What do you know about offices?" I asked her. But she always had an answer. Like Prins. "A place that is neat," she said. For her, an office was where everything has its correct place, people plan their whole day and you have a job to do. Where she got the idea from I don't know. Not from her father. Jason was never like that. But that girl wanted to be part of a telephone company. Or a hospital.' Pearl had clapped her hands. 'I said, "Good. That is wonderful. If you can get a job, you can be independent. I think that is *galkissa*-wonderful." But I warned her, even an office can be full of rubbish, and men who are idiots.'

Anoja had set about her career methodically. She first registered with a secretarial school and started to learn shorthand and typing. She worked resolutely and completed her course with plaudits. Within a year she was in a job in the City, working for a private firm involved with the Far East: rubber, tea, commodities.

But Pearl wished Anoja would show some sign of her distinctiveness; she felt a knot tighten in her degaussed womb. 'I wished she would show some emotion, you know.' Pearl slowly sipped her sherry. '"Why don't you wear a sari one day to the office. A nice, smart sari?" I asked. But she was horrified. "They'd love it," I said.

"People love to see something different, you know." But she was adamant. "Not these days, *Amma*. There's quite enough difference around as it is." She always dressed conventionally for her London office: dark skirt cut to the season's length, a stiff neat blouse, black hard shoes. My God, she walked with a click you could measure a clock by.' Pearl paused to watch a Black Magic advertisement on the TV. 'Look at him,' she pointed. 'Love and chocolate,' she smiled.

'One day she brought home a box from Fortnum & Mason. I had not seen those pink fondants since Jason bought me a box when we first came here. "You bought these?" I asked her. It was so unlike that child.' Pearl rummaged around her knitting basket looking for a handkerchief. 'I'll never forget her smile that day: so fresh that her face seemed to sail. It was like she had turned sixteen again. She said Bernard had given them.'

o

On November 11th 1964, Anoja married Bernard at the registry office of a London borough. 'No church and no party. She had not changed that much. It was just that this Bernard was meant to be *different*.' Pearl suppressed a smile

92

from blowing open her lips. 'All I know is that it was only after he came on the scene that she started talking to me – like a daughter to a mother. But I have to say I never quite warmed to this Bernard. Bernard.'

'Your sister has married a Bernard,' she had written to Prins as though the syllables of the name itself signified something – the way Ducal at home was rooted in *dhukha*, sadness, or Vatunas in the fallen. 'Can you imagine? He has a house in Sussex and they will live out in the country. If you are lucky you might get to see the inside of a real English castle when you come.'

But Prins never did see Anoja in her husband's 'castle'. Pearl was not ready for him to come to England, or perhaps England was not ready for him, for a few more years, by which time it was too late. He never saw her truly happy.

Bernard had been an executive in the same firm that Anoja worked at. He had been out to Malaya, as it was then, and been quite taken with the heat and deep-green trees, the warm sap he found in his veins. When he came back to England, he was disorientated.

But Anoja had told Pearl that he was the most fascinating man in the building. One of the few people in that conventional office who seemed to find time to joke and talk about the destinations of their mail with the casual knowledge of a man of the world. In the summer he wore a tropical linen suit to show that he had been to places his colleagues knew only as postmarks, and ties from Carnaby Street.

'He could be quite a prankster,' Pearl admitted. 'One afternoon, he had returned to the office late after the lunch hour. The sun was streaming in through the open windows. It was summer. Anoja could hear riverboats on the Thames as though the whole place had been transported to a hot country. Bernard had sauntered into her room where she normally sat with three other girls. On this day, apparently, the others were away. One on leave, another sick and the third flirting somewhere. The fellow then produced a small yellow orchid for her. Anoja said it was just like those yellow limpets we used to have up-country. Bernard had said that he had ordered it especially from a garden in Johore. She believed him for a moment, but then he started laughing and confessed that he had stolen it from the orchid house in Kew Gardens. No one had ever treated her so irreverently before in her life.'

o

By the time Prins first came to England, Anoja had died giving birth to Naomi. Both of us, Naomi and I, came into the world the same way, losing someone even with the first breath. Bernard had remarried and Naomi had become part of another family. They had moved to Manchester where Bernard had found a new position; his experience of foreign trade and Britain's far-flung enterprises were highly valued at the time and it was relatively easy to become a colonial retread. Naomi would be brought to meet her grandmother occasionally and then, in her teens, Naomi would visit Pearl on her own. Prins met her from time to time but didn't ever get to know Bernard. Not even while he was up in Oldham.

Pearl also never visited Bernard in his new life. There was no need. There were two different countries – Bernard's and Anoja's – and there had only been one overlapping segment: finite and circumscribed and over. An arena beyond which nobody seemed to stray. Naomi was the only one who knew no boundaries, or seemed to cross wherever she wished, and whenever she wished.

V

THREE O'CLOCK

Maria sashayed back to the table on the crest of an unnerving smile. 'Guys all right? Want anything?' Mister Moon's was beginning to empty.

I looked at Prins. 'Another beer?'

He declined demurely, like a boy hiding his hormones, his head full of home.

'Coffee? Cappuccino?'

I tried to find out more about what Prins was up to in Colombo. 'What's so important that you have to be back for Monday?'

Prins pulled out his lower lip with his thumb and forefinger, then let it go slowly. 'It's big business now, you know. You have to be on the ball: *go, go, go* all the time.' His own peppy words fired him up.

'But I guess even for my father it was like that. The successful Jason Ducal *mahattheya* would have been pretty busy calculating the shipping routes around the world; even before Suez he always planned for contingencies. Shooting off telegrams in the middle of the night. "A for alpha, B for beta, C for Ceylon . . . sea-lawn, *men*." He was a busy man. He knew his business. He seemed to have been so good at knowing what was coming. Being prepared. But I hardly ever saw him; he hardly ever saw me. A lot of *busy*ness going on even in our sleepy old town. That was when the big shots were laying down all these bloody laws of self-interest, you know. The rules by which we have been stomping over each other for forty years. But I was only a kid and wouldn't have known what the fuck it was all about. Now I am having to reconstruct the whole con-certina: nothing remembered, nothing forgotten and everything up for grabs.'

'But,' I interjected, 'why do you want to rush so much. Is it Lola? Did you call her?'

Prins took a deep breath and rubbed his eyes. 'It's all so hazy, but sometimes it seems I can remember more than I thought I could. D'you know what I mean? Now I can remember battling with the six-times tables – blue lines, red lines – and making piccies of prick-headed elephants. My teacher's note to my father: "Prins is not an unintelligent boy, but he is lazy. He appears to have great difficulty with

97

his tables." The teacher was a cow, but Papa kept this moronic letter in the house. Maybe he planned to find time to teach me the six-times table. Maybe he was going to blast the Headshyster about the teacher. Or maybe he never even looked at it, he was so busy being a bloody businessman.'

Prins leaned forward and cupped his hands to make a miniature theatre. 'Imagine his study. Full of rubbish: folders and files bursting with notes and letters. No one is allowed even a peek. The Bridge is up there. I sneak in one day when he has gone on a trip to some estate. It is so claustrophobic, in spite of all the windows. It's like a fish tank. I can't even breathe in there, you know. But behind the samovar I find a stack of *Playboy*s. My first glimpse: Marilyn Monroe without her clothes . . . The man had really got everything he could ever have wanted. In his early forties he had achieved all his top ambitions: a first-class job, this great big house, a family. And yet, he seemed hooked to the business of being busy, acquiring things day and night. If he had been paid by the hour, he would have been a billionaire.

'The firm had grown into one of the best-connected newly lionized companies. Top-bracket, our fellows who put their money in to get a place on the new Board. He was already on the top landing: a Director. Things were changing, you know. He was the one who was taking the company into the new world. The World Bank report in 1952 said that the business sector needed to be "unleashed". That was him. He was the one they saw really straining at the leash.

'By 1956, the year he died, he had a plan to rejuvenate the whole beverages business, including our bloody *pol-katu* booze. He wanted to take his firm into domestic liquor; he'd had enough of pandering to the Lipton's and Brooke Bonds of this world. He wanted our people to have some pride in what they produced and generate wealth from the home base. Be world-class *at home*. I found a newspaper article about him – written before he died – praising him to the hilt for his responsible mix of business acumen and ethical considerations. "A welcome contrast to some of our other big-time businessmen and party-time politicians," it said. You can imagine how that went down with old Esra Vatunas next door and the business buffoons of the day. Those were the days when every politician seemed to have a party; and no party had a real, responsible politician.

'Although he was rarely at home, Papa couldn't have been completely absent from the matrimonial bed in those years, could he? After all, there was Ravi – fallen like an angel from heaven. But when I first started looking into it all years ago, before I went back, it seemed so unclear. I was getting nowhere fast, you know. There was nothing of the man in our flat here. And then, when I tried to find out about our lives back home, it was like swimming in treacle. I didn't know where to start. How to find out anything? The entire bloody country seems to have always been one big barrel of rumour and conspiracy.

'When I got there in '81, one of the first things I did was visit Arcadia. It felt incredibly familiar: the grain of the wood, the powdery plaster, the smell of cold floor-polish. The German couple living there – two tiddly aid officials – opened all the doors for me. But it was difficult to connect to it. Despite the recognition, there didn't seem to be anything there for me. Then more recently, when I started visiting Lola next door, I began to feel more of a pull, you know. Maybe because it was empty by then: no hint of life in it. The garden was a dump, and the old house looked like a shipwreck. The place had been abandoned for some reason. Fortunately Lola's brother Dino is renovating it now.' Prins paused, letting the picture of Arcadia settle.

'The only clue to the past I found was Sunderam, the old gardener. But he is so ancient now. Can't see very well, can't hear very well, and talks cock. He has been at Bellevue for decades. I guess ever since *Amma* – we – left. He had nowhere else to go. I tried to find out something about our time in Arcadia from him, but I couldn't really get much sense out of him. He just droned on and on. All that seemed important to him was the time that *Amma* asked him to destroy the mussaenda hedge at the side of the garden. He had put so much into it: love, compassion, a weekly dose of horse manure, but she had wanted it cut down for light. She apparently had a thing about the dark edges of the garden, and this hedge ran right up along the side of the house, by the bedroom window. Sunderam was almost whimpering just remembering that.

'So you see, I don't know what to make of it all. There's my mother, Anoja, Ravi and me with one Vatunas – Esra – digging the earth and trying to eject us out of his sight, and another, his son Tivoli – Lola's father – dreaming like this was a real arcadia. And Papa-boy is perfecting his truly indigenous engine of growth, ignoring them and us. What is he up to? Our fly-by-night leaders are frolicking with half-naked champagne girls, but money seems to be all Papa wants. Money, money, money. Why? Does he want to buy out the old reptile Esra? I don't know. *Amma* would have known, if anybody did. But she never told anyone, not even us, her own children. And after he died, she seemed to have wiped his presence out of her life. Now she too has gone and the truth of that time has vanished forever.'

Prins had never talked much about his father, Jason, until that last time we met. It was as if Pearl was the one who had shaped the whole Ducal family, despite Jason stamping his name on her progeny. But that was changing, hour by hour.

O

'What about Esra himself?' He was the one I was most curious about from what Pearl had told me of those early skirmishes. 'Did you ever talk to him?'

'Bugger died years ago. Nobody shed any tears about that. A real bastard, although you'd think he'd be a hero these days for making the unscrupulous so respectable. His own father thought he was a shit. Lola calls him a mutant. Her grandmother, Esra's wife, was sweet as apple-pie but he never even spoke to her. Lola blames him for destroying her father.'

Prins spooned a heap of sugar into his cup and watched the mound sink in an inverted pyramid through the muddy froth. He told me what he knew about Esra and the rest of the Vatunases, gleaned from Lola – the one and only Vatunas who seemed able to speak without rancour or an eye on future gains – and the gossip of a small town break-ing into the big-time.

In his seventy-two years Esra had made many enemies and no friends. His wealth was legendary, but rarely manifested

itself except in grit and private property. While his contemporaries emulated the vanities of their pre-war colonial
masters, trying to transform themselves into brownskin
imperial successors, Esra turned himself into a full-blown
emperor. He had a small army of lawyers and accountants
constantly working for him. 'His main office was run like a
military camp,' Prins snapped his fingers. 'When he arrived
the peons would salute; his Chief Accountant would stand
at attention, his Legal Advisor would waddle behind him
like a pigeon with a brief under his wing.' Even in his later
years – Esra never completely released his grip – he would
go to the office every morning and ensure that his troops
were ready for the day's new battles. Each man and woman
knew what to do: his or her small part in the greater plan of
the Emperor, but nobody but Esra knew the whole plan.

'Unlike his father, Esra's original dynastic ambition was
to create a *subtle* empire which would be fully appreciated
and understood only by himself.' Prins believed that Esra
did not want his success displayed to the rest of the country.
Those who worked for him he impressed by his control
over their ignorance; those whom he regarded as influential
he impressed by whatever impressed them most: cunning,
mystery, gems, capital, baffling income, mind-boggling sex,
prime land and the uncontrollable, unknowable expansion
of an empire under their feet. He was shrewd and econom-
ical; he wanted efficiency in every effort.

As Tivoli was his only child, the intricacies of his financial holdings became as arcane as the orders of an overblown religious sect. The empire he constructed waited for Tivoli to bring forth his heirs and when he did, the whole web of invisible dealings leaped across the ledgers of a dozen companies to create another fantastic web of dependence, independence and secreted fortunes. But no one single part knew the full extent of the whole, nor the extent of the knowledge of any other part, except old Esra himself. Alone. The only omniscient one in the Vatunas universe.

Esra took enormous visible pleasure from these machinations. His eyes would light up whenever any of his business associates expressed surprise at one or another of his dealings. He even liked to set up false trails for his own accountants and lawyers to follow. 'It was all a game for him' Prins concluded, 'an immensely important game. Even Tivoli never quite got the measure of the old man's schemes.'

o

Tivoli was known around town as a rake but one with none of the rapacity that gleamed out of his father's mouth.

His involvement with women had started late but was always conducted with considerable style in an otherwise graceless world.

Tivoli had drifted for much of his life and looked in a daze most of the time, unless an attractive woman gladdened his eye. Although he joined the clubs of the previous era without much consideration, his only real occupation for a long time was in capturing an alluring figure in one way or another.

'He made small smutty drawings that looked like cosmic thumbprints, and sketches of nudes in sultry poses. But early in the fifties, Tivoli stopped drawing so compulsively. His sketches turned macabre: Don Quixote falling off a horse buggering Death; a dismembered human head licked by a lion.' Prins said that Tivoli had started smoking cigarettes – Player's Navy Cut – at about that time. He became more tense.

Tivoli's mother, Delia, kept telling him that Esra had become much mellower, but her appeals did not move Tivoli; he did not like the sourness of the spirits that curdled his father's lair. He would insist he had nothing to say and bow out of the way. He had sons to perform his filial duties in a neat generational sleight of hand. They could speak with his voice to their grandfather and find an echo in his head, a self-seeking loop in a recalcitrant gene coiled and preserved in the brine of his old age.

Then on Good Friday 1953, the day Ravi Ducal was born on the other side of the hedgerow, Tivoli Vatunas decided he should become more like his father. 'He spent most of the morning upstairs in his room, away from the daily bustle of the household. His two older sons, Kia and Dino, were at school. Sita, his wife, had the morning's shopping to do from Friday's vendors, as and when they came to the house, and had planned to take her toddler, Buppy, to visit some friends before going to the zoo when the day cooled a little, if it did.'

Tivoli was sweating in a blue sarong and a white mesh singlet. He never wore anything else when he was in his room and he rarely emerged from there into the rest of the house, or out of the house, before about four o'clock in the afternoon. After having his regular breakfast of reddish stringhoppers and fish curry on the terrace, he settled down with his grandfather's pen and wrote a letter to his father.

He was brief. He said he was now ready to take his place in the Vatunas scheme of things. To prove his worth he had observed for some time, on the sly, the business methods of his father and his troops. 'You may not have noticed,' he had written, 'but your accountant and your legal adviser are incompetent. They are far too complacent and serve only their own interests.' He also advised Esra that at this point in his life he should concentrate on his true place in the world and let his son shoulder the burden of running the business and perhaps even expanding it into new areas.

'When Esra received the letter at lunchtime he exploded,' Prins banged the table. '"The little shrimp has some spunk," Esra waves the letter in front of Delia. "Look, those balls of his have finally pumped some brains into the fellow's head." His face opens in the shape of a scythe. Delia wags her head happily. "He is your son, no? A real Vatunas boy."

'But back in his own house, Tivoli Vatunas sat alone. The letter had been delivered by hand. He was thirty-eight years old and on the brink of something new.'

Tivoli had been brooding all his life. On this day, something inside him that had lain dormant, like an unfertilized egg, suddenly seemed to have been activated. The smoke in his head cleared and his father's presence receded into that of an old man sitting in an armchair on a veranda. Everything that had been Esra's now appeared to Tivoli as his own.

'When the call came from his father, Tivoli was ready. He had changed into a starched white shirt and a pair of trousers fresh from the laundry in anticipation.' Prins paused. 'Esra Vatunas was on the back veranda. Delia was there too, flushed with pride. "Good,"' Prins clicked his teeth rapidly, imitating Esra.

'Tivoli sat down and said nothing at first. He looked steadily at his father in a way he never had before. This time it was his father who seemed unable to hold his gaze, and whose eyes kept slipping out of line. "All right," Esra, gruff as *gultik*, conceded. "We'll start on Monday. Come to the office and we'll see about these incompetent staff you talk about."

'Tivoli had risen. "No. We'll start now." Then he proceeded to tell Esra how his accountant had missed two important items in the last tax return which would have cost Esra half a per cent in his profits, and how his legal adviser was simply using textbook procedures and not thinking creatively about the way his last acquisition was incorporated. His cost accounting was apparently first-class.'

Delia had left them talking and waltzed happily inside. The voices of the two Vatunas men in her life was the duet she had been longing to hear.

o

'Three years later, in 1956, Esra made his boldest commercial move. He had spent eighteen months planning it; an unprecedented campaign in the economic history of the island. You know, before that we had none of these muscle-man takeovers you get now. People stuck to their place. Niche marketing – that was all that ever happened. Esra was our first real commercial predator.' Prins lowered his voice, 'You see, he was a button-arsed power freak. He wanted to control the state of the whole nation, head and bowels. "The British had spread drunkenness into the hills," you remember Governor Gregory's old joke? Eighty years later, Esra wanted to ladle it out into every nook and cranny.' Esra Vatunas had set his sights on a small but troubled distillery that had a production plant for local gin and coconut arrack a few miles out of Colombo. The company had its origins in the arrack rents procured by Ambrose Budego at the turn of the century. With Independence in 1948, Ambrose Budego & Son was licensed as the smallest of a dozen private legal distilleries operating in the country.

But by the early 1950s it was not doing well. Ambrose Budego's son blamed the downturn on the lack of a nationalist taste amongst the country's political leadership, who drank only Scotch, and the fiasco of trying to introduce communalism into the art of toddy-tapping – the high-wire collection of the palm-flower juice for fermenting into arrack. But Esra believed this was a temporary problem and that a boom for a fine local spirit couldn't be held back for long.

'"The Minister for Industry calls for more roof tiles, but

what this country really needs is a top-drawer hooch in a sexpot bottle," Esra had claimed. "We can produce our own Coconut Caresser and Sheet Twister with a dash of lime and a *hakuru* cut."'

Esra reckoned on arrack, as had the forefathers of his wealthiest contemporaries. 'All the big families of the colonial era, like the colonial era itself, did well out of stupor,' Prins contended. 'While they tried to disguise the stink of raw *ra* with Chanel No. 5, Esra wanted to dive right into it. If he had another son, a suitably arranged marriage into the toxy trade would have been the most economic option, but Tivoli was already gartered and Esra's grandsons would be zipping their pips much too late. The best he could do now was to get Tivoli, with his new-found commercial zeal, to procure an ailing distillery for a knock-down price.' Prins took a deep rush of a breath. Like Pearl, he loved to dramatize his stories.

'But then, on the afternoon that Tivoli was preparing his final proposal for the Budego bid, the new Vatunas Chief Accountant, Lionel Samarasekera, had scurried over. He saluted Esra on his veranda.' Prins demonstrated the action at Bellevue nearly forty years earlier, using only a Mister Moon's cup and saucer for a prop.

'"What?" Esra barked.

'"Sir, there is a storm brewing."'

'Esra said nothing, but looked at the man as though he was an imbecile. *Storm?* He would have known that Parliament had been dissolved, but he would not have expected that to affect his immaculate plan.

'"Sir, it may only be in a teacup for now, but I am given to understand that the Sanderson Bros. company is doing some serious connection with the Ambrose Budego concern."

'Esra nearly killed Lionel that afternoon. When he had finally loosened his grip on Lionel's bruised throat, Lionel only managed to squeak, "Advance warning, sir. No fault of mine own, sir. Only advance warning."'

Prins explained that the Budego company was essential to Esra's grand plan for transforming his capital from land to liquid; to free him from the constraints of the inevitable development of equitable land-reform policies, future strictures on the expansionist tendencies of individuals like himself, and from business bloody inertia. Esra had read about Winston Churchill's conversion to whisky and realized that if the traditional pot-arrack was to be blended with a lighter alcohol it could have a wider social appeal among the moneyed classes. At the Coconut Exhibition he had noticed a very passable coconut brandy. But no one else seemed interested.

'Although consumption of arrack had trebled, and trebled again, in the transition from colonial rule to

111

Independence, there was thought to be no real market for a more expensively produced arrack at the time: wealthier tipplers preferred to ally themselves to more exotic foreign liquor even if it was the cheapest, nastiest, daft horse-piss of an imported whisky.' Prins lifted his coffee cup and sniffed it. 'Arrack smelled bad to the rich in those days, ignorant of their own natural scent. But Esra was thinking ten years ahead.'

'But what about all that prohibition talk that went on at the time?' I asked. 'Wasn't that when people were getting excited again about religion?'

'All that "freedom through temperance" business had dried up. They were dead slogans. Whisky was cheap. The only argument was the old one about foreign pollution, but it was too late by then. The talk only stoked up the thirst.' Prins grinned. 'Esra was very sharp. He saw how a new drink could really make big bucks – boom or bust. He is the one who came up with the idea: *Vam*brosia. A pukka blend, I have to say. A Vatunas mixer with the mask of old Ambrose. Esra knew it would be a colossal winner. To lose his opportunity to intoxicate all our crapulous heads for years to come was too apocalyptic for Esra to contemplate. Especially if he was to lose to a company represented by my father: the enemy whose house had its backside shoved right in his face.'

Esra had dismissed Lionel and called for a team of fixers.

He instructed them to concoct a story for the morning paper that would expose a potential link between a sexually debilitating nervous disorder and Ambrose Budego's staple liquor. 'He wanted to put a real scare on. He planned to mend the damage later by sacrificing some hack and getting him to confess, at a price, his responsibility for the scaremongering. But only once Esra was in control of the Budego enterprise and ready to relaunch the bottle with a really sexy label.'

The next day's headlines ran true to form: arrack was portrayed as suicidal. Not only did it lead to a life of crime and delinquency but also to sterility and testicular problems. Even the more upmarket gin was said to lighten the blood so that it rose to the head and drained the loins of any strength. The panic affected all the distilleries. All over the island production slowed down; the country's taverners and imbibers held their breath and anxiously tested each other's fast-wilting libidos. Letters to the newspapers complained about the catastrophic effects of hard-drinking on soft noses and weak organs. A famous film-star confession was featured in the illustrated Sunday supplement as 'Cocktails: My Aphrodisaster.' Questions were raised as to whether the hazard was peculiar to Budego products, or whether it might be common to all local liquor, perhaps even imported liquor. The temperance movement was dumbfounded: should we have combated wickedness with

lust all this time? Or was this divine retribution from
another faith?

o

'OK. Now imagine Arcadia. My father pacing up and down
his garden. From his veranda, old man Esra would have
heard twigs snap like gunshots. My father is furious with his
firm for dithering over his carefully arranged bond with
Budego, just because of an old distaste for the tavern trade
and foolishly sensational newspapering. He is even more
furious with his Chairman for his hopeless snobbishness.

'I think my father really believed that if they didn't take
the distilleries into their group, it would be a major blow
against the future survival of Sanderson Bros. This was to be
the first tentative exploration of the concept of diversifica-
tion, which he believed he had invented. He wanted the firm
to diversify its interests from brewing high-class two-leaves-
and-a-bud tea to inebriating with firewater of the finest kind.'

A workaday version of the principle that imperious businessmen like Esra used to diversify their sources of enduring
wealth. And Jason, like Esra, clearly believed that alcohol
had a permanent economic role to play whatever the future
of the island.

'I think he must have suspected a plot in the way the newspaper story had broken; but he couldn't, as yet, trace the connections. It was the luck of the dogs,' Prins said.

'His Chairman, Eddy Kaduwira, was a cocky old man who was in the firm because of the usual butt-head family connection rather than business acumen. The idea that the newspaper story was only a rumour put out by a rival who hoped to get Sanderson Bros. to behave exactly the way they were doing, would be unimaginable to the old fart.' Prins stuck a rolled-up serviette on his upper lip like a moustache. '"This is so far fetched, old chap," the fellow would have scoffed. "Who would be so interested in this *thraada* business? Those fellows have been shimmying up coconut trees for donkey's years, why would anybody else want to scrub their goolies up there now?" My father wouldn't have known about Esra's interest but he would have said that arrack has been extremely lucrative for a hundred years, so someone must be. It was the only route to real capital accumulation: cheap to produce, and a permanently addicted market. Why do you think the British introduced these taverns? It's like the opium dens.'

I too could imagine how the argument between Jason and his Chairman might have gone.

'But what if this libido business is true, old chap? Who would lie about a thing like that?'

'I don't know who, but the reason I can imagine.'

'That is your trouble, Jason. Your fertile imagination. You would be better off putting it into some other use, in the bedroom rather than the Boardroom perhaps,' Eddy Kaduwira sniggered. *'Give up this bloody arrack, man. Give it up.'*

o

'A few months ago, Ranil and Mira had their fifth anniversary party.' Prins wiped the bubbles of cappuccino froth off his upper lip, 'You remember Mira, don't you?'

'I do, I do,' I said. How could I not remember Mira, my Mira, who went and married Ranil for some incomprehensible reason.

'*Fuck*,' was the first word she ever said to me. She was hopping about on Pearl's doorstep waiting for Prins to open the door. She had lost the heel of one of her purple boots. 'I want to fly.' Her eyes widened, her mouth opened like a beak. 'Fly, fly, fly out of this cheap, cheap town.' She didn't even know my name and it was already in her mouth. She crouched down, half sinking, disappearing into her own shoulders. For one delirious moment the sense of flight – the flapping of wings – seemed everywhere in the air. She wore a purple hat squashed down over her ears. The broken suede boots seemed to be trying to achieve the same effect with her feet, but upside down. There were feathers stitched into the seams of her jeans, even in her crotch.

Mira came from a distinguished Colombo family – her father was an eminent judge – and this was her way of expressing her personality and developing a fresh identity. She was another one who liked to keep her distance from her family. She had been sent to study law in London, but had given that up and had become a sales assistant in a South Molton Street boutique. She claimed that swearing out of hours was the only antidote to the enforced politeness of her daily work and her Pygmalion childhood, besides public fornication. After work she only restrained herself when she stepped inside Pearl's flat, where we would congregate every couple of months – Christmas, Easter, May Day, Whitsun – for Pearl's heart-warming *buth* curry.

Mira loved to be different. Hell for her would have been meeting someone dressed like herself. Or home. Or worst of all, both together. In an age where conformity ruled even among the most nonconformist, Mira stood out like a sore thumb. Painted red, blue and black like a bruise. And by the time these colours of pain became the fashion, she would have moved on: magenta and puce, mud and silage, ash and potash.

'Anyway,' Prins continued sipping his cappuccino, 'at this gigantic do at the Ramada, I met a man called Mohan Jayasuriya. Tight as a tick. But he knew who I was and he grabbed me. He held me like a skywalker with vertigo. "Why you not drinking, man?" He got hold of two drinks, stiff bloody Black Arracks, and insisted on my downing one. He blathered on about my father. "I knew him, shonne," he said. "I am show sherry." "He's been dead nearly forty years," I said. "What's the sorry about now?" So he leans towards me and says, "You know shonne, your father believed in this shtuff. Sho did I. But what to do? . . . It was a shtory." The bugger tips his shoulders and tells me, "What could I do? It was a story."' Prins looked up at Mister Moon's galactic ceiling, his eyes rolling back in his head.

'This guy has been sucking the bottle for at least two years, probably forty-two years. He couldn't even stand. He was holding onto my shoulder. Fat grin on his face like he's pissing in the rain. "What are you telling me," I asked him and he looks at me in a real puzzle, like Yogi Bear: *Me?* "What story?" I ask. *"Shtory?"* Prins said that Mohan Jayasuriya kept looking at him and wiggling his head like he had a fly in his ear.

Ranil had come up and explained to Prins that Mohan Jayasuriya was a man who knew exactly what he wanted out of life. He had given up a career at one of the top newspapers in the land to go and live in the blissful peace of the hills of the Central Province. 'Isn't that so, uncle?'

Mohan Jayasuriya had looked at Ranil in stupefied disbelief. 'Yesh,' he had confessed. 'Yesh.' Then, lunging forward for another drink, he had lost his balance and crashed down through a glass-topped table onto the floor.

Prins had rolled him over on his back, convinced that yet another lead to the past was now beyond his reach. The man had gone down with such force that the table was smashed to smithereens. A splinter had ripped his hand and there was blood spurting out from between the torn ligaments of his fingers onto his shirt.

Mira, brandishing a pineapple wand, had shrieked out, 'Fucking hell,' which left many of her family friends and in-laws almost as stunned as Mohan Jayasuriya.

'It's OK,' Prins had said. He was not dead; not even unconscious. Just drunk. Too drunk to say another word.

'For the last thirty years he has been up-country,' Ranil had apologized as Mohan was being carried out. 'He still does some writing, but it is only a letter column for the Planter's Association newsletter. Otherwise he works at a small tea estate, rinsing his mouth out with turpentine every night.'

'An old Sanderson Bros. estate?' Prins had asked, trying to close a gap in the pattern that was forming in his mind.

'No, a Vatunas outfit.'

Prins had discovered that not only was Mohan Jayasuriya a fallen journalist, but also a distant relative of the Vatunases through marriage.

Ranil had not known any more about the man or his link with Jason Ducal; he had said his mother probably knew his whole history.

'I could suddenly see what might have happened in the whole arrack business,' Prins tapped the centre of his palm with one finger as if to show me. 'All night I couldn't sleep. At last I had found the guy who had set it all up.'

The next day Prins had gone to Ranil's mother's house.

o

She lived in a smart bungalow with money plants growing around the walls. 'Chinese doors, ornate fretwork, a marble room, and there: Ranil's mama languishing with a pile of glossy magazines from Hong Kong.'

'Very nice party, aunty,' Prins had greeted her.

'My, but what a commotion with that Mohan, no? Who invited him? Such a good-for-nothing fellow, no?'

Prins had asked her whether she knew him before he became a tea planter.

'Not a tea planter, he just works for the tea company,

120

darling. More lush than planter. They say he is always loafing about in one bar or another.'

'And before that,' he had persisted. 'He was trying to tell me something about my father and some drink . . .'

'Yes, darling, our Jason was quite fond of a drink too, wasn't he? But this fellow used to work for the *Daily Watch* and then got it into some big trouble. He had to leave. I am sure it too was to do with drinking.'

Prins had not been able to get any more useful information out of her; all she had done was run the man down.

'Anyway, what does it matter, darling? The way he behaved last night, I think you can safely say that the less you know of him the better. But Ranil and Mira looked so nice, didn't they?'

'Yes,' Prins had agreed, wildly hoping for a last clue.

'Only thing is that girl is so highly strung, she sometimes says the most . . . odd things, no? I never thought my little Ranil would ever go for someone with such . . . *vivid* language.'

O

The day Mohan Jayasuriya had resigned from his newspaper the lead editorial had been tremendously stirring: a fierce attack on the unscrupulousness of the new fanatical wing of the traditional temperance movement, which had stooped to rumour-mongering and deliberate misinformation, resulting in one of the paper's younger, more gullible, reporters losing his head. 'Mohan Jayasuriya found himself footloose – but handsomely pensioned – for about twelve months, until this surprisingly pukka position looking over the tea-tops of Central Province suddenly opened for him.' Prins clicked his fingers like a magician.

'Next time I found him was at The Cool Kurumba.' A regular watering hole for out-of-towners, famous for its gaudy murals of pink coconut palms fronting a viridescent ocean, and a barman who had the face of Bruce Lee tattooed on his arm.

'How's the hand?' Prins had asked.

Mohan Jayasuriya's hand was covered in gauze and hanging from a sling. A small strawberry patch grew near the valley of his thumb and forefinger.

'I keep wanting to go for the glass with this hand, *men*. Funny how used to it you get, no? Using the same hand. Napoleon-like, huh?'

Prins had bought him another drink, and a pineapple juice for himself.

'You said you were a newspaperman,' Prins had prompted.

'Did I say that?'

'At the Ramada. You were in newspapers before tea. Isn't that right?'

Mohan had looked glum. He had emptied his glass. He had seemed to need the drink to release the cord knotted in his throat. 'I was twenty-two,' he had mumbled. 'I wrote brilliant copy. I wanted to be an investigative reporter, like Jimmy Stewart in what's-its-name. Ever see that movie? Brilliant. But what I thought was going to be my big break, turned out to be my last story.'

Prins had bought him another drink.

'I should have known. I was fed this stupid line about how Budego's arrack had this stuff in it that made your dick go dinky – phut. I believed it. I went crazy. Impotent. I tried everything. Took Sextogen by the carton. I'd have drunk cockroach juice, if they said it would fix it. But nothing doing: it was floppy as a pickled herring. What the hell happened, I don't know. Almost forty years now and not even a dribble. No hint of another story ever.'

Mohan Jayasuriya had looked over his glass and told Prins, 'Letters now. That's what I write. Letters on nature, pastoral letters, letters of regret, even love . . . You getting married? You want a letter for your beloved? Something to remember how you got her into bed? The first jolly-jolly. Just tell me. I'll do it for you gratis. Al fresco. A little bit of Kama Sutra in the perfumed garden. Just give me a few details, the dimensions . . .'

After another swig, Mohan Jayasuriya had leant closer to Prins and whispered, 'Your father was a good man, you know.'

'You knew him?' Prins had tried to encourage him without frightening him with his eagerness.

'No, I did not know him. No, no, no. But I wish I had, ashually. Afterwards I realized that. I should have liked to have been able to tell him what had happened.'

Prins said that Mohan Jayasuriya was a man who seemed to have an ever diminishing window of coherence in his conversation. He could never go beyond his starting point and say what was in his head. To pursue a point was impossible. He was like an exhausted man throwing a ball up in the air. Each throw became weaker and weaker, and each time the ball's arc became shorter and shorter. Until at last nothing moved: the ball barely left his hand, the words his mouth. His torrid planter's letters must have been as punch-packed as a used skin.

'But I checked the files,' Prins tapped the table with his coffee spoon like a schoolmaster. 'My father died three weeks before that story of Jayasuriya's was exposed as a hoax, you know. My father and Eddy Kaduwira, his Chairman, both died at the same time. Right in the middle of the biggest election campaign to date. The liquor business was in *schtuk*. The monks mad about Jayanti – the biggest Buddhist event in 2500 years – the toddy tappers'

124

season due to cause havoc. Calls for prohibition, and the whole country without a single hard-on. A real *pol-mallum*. In these three weeks Sanderson Bros. drifts away from the liquor business and Esra Vatunas bails out Ambrose Budego & Son. What d'you think of that?' He slurped the last of his coffee, and I paid the bill.

VI

QUARTER TO FIVE

When we came out of Mister Moon's, the sun had withdrawn. The winter's chill rushed into the dark space left behind. Prins was shivering. 'Jesus,' he said. 'Is it going to snow or something?'

The iciness of the air seemed to pierce our lungs with each breath. 'It's like breathing bloody stalactites,' Prins complained.

We headed back towards my place. The antique shop across the road had a candelabra lit with eight tall church candles. I could see an old woman's wrinkled, yellow face staring out at us from the shop as we hurried past in the cold.

Prins suddenly stopped. 'Can you smell it?'

As he said it, I too noticed a peculiar pungency to the exhausted air of our urban vale. Wood smoke? A winter barbecue?

'Something's burning,' he looked at me apprehensively.

'It's all these renovated Victorian fireplaces,' I suggested. 'This place is a throwback to the past, everybody wants to pretend they live in a time machine. They want Sainsbury's fresh fruit and yesterday's warm wood glow all in the same room, twelve minutes from the West End . . .'

'I think it's a big fire,' Prins interrupted. 'Look at the sky over there. A fire bomb?'

There was a glow rising above the houses pitched against the hill, as if the sun had left behind a slowly fading rimmark. Prins started up the road.

'Wait,' I called out. 'Where are you going?'

'Come on. We should see what it is.' Prins raced ahead.

I wanted to say, What's there to see? I was feeling cold now that the sun had gone. I wanted to go home. But he was already halfway up the hill. Prins was always on the lookout, always wanting to find things out. I preferred to let things be, but everyone seems to want to tell me everything. I soak it in and don't let anything out until it is too late. There was never the right moment to tell Prins all that Pearl had said to me.

Grey flakes swirled in the air like snow. 'It's ash,' Prins held out his hand and rubbed his bare, freezing fingers together.

At the top we turned left along the ridge and walked down an alleyway, until we reached a playground full of people gawping at the old railway warehouses ablaze in the valley below. A jumble of railway lines seemed to writhe in the flames around the disused shunting station.

'Look, I told you,' Prins's voice trembled. 'I could smell it. I knew it was something big. Must be the IRA.'

The building at the end burst into flames. It had been like a shadow behind the others; suddenly the roof caved in and flames leapt out of its centre. It hissed and spluttered in an explosion of pinwheels. What had been there was now gone forever.

The crowd cheered.

Thick black smoke spread in a dense cloud, rising from a huge blaze. In the flames you could see small speckled tornadoes rise to feed the cloud as though they were helping the sky itself turn blacker for the night. Most of the warehouses in front were completely engulfed in flames. Huge robes of yellow and orange swirled; only the frame of the building stayed in a stencilled afterlife providing a temporary structure for the flames. Then the beams splintered and crackled into a yellow emptiness.

In the distance the firefighters looked like toy figurines. Their puny jets of water moving in and out like the whiskers of some pyromaniacal giant insect feeling its way to the centre of the heat.

A fourth fire engine drew up on the far side of the furnace and spilled its little team of men and hoses to stop the fire from creeping up the railway tracks.

I looked at Prins; he was standing ahead of me, a little closer to the fire. Perhaps only one yard out of a thousand, but still one yard closer. From where I was standing, Prins's eyes looked watery; the film of a tear, like a firefighter's protective douche, made them glisten in the glare of the huge furnace below us. His mouth was slightly open. I could see him press his tongue against his teeth. 'How did it start?' Prins asked nervously. Someone answered, 'Vandals.' Another joined in by saying they were empty warehouses ready for demolition.

'Prins,' I called. 'Let's go back.' He didn't seem to hear me. He seemed entranced. I called him again.

'Wait,' his voice full of relief and growing wonder. 'This is amazing. Look at how it burns.' As he spoke the struts of another building collapsed in a spray of flames. 'Beautiful,' he whispered as if he had never seen a building on fire before, despite the inferno back home.

A small huddle of boys nearby cheered again. A man with a baby in a pushchair began to unbuckle the baby's harness. He was cooing as he lifted the baby, face towards the flames. 'Fire, fire,' he was chanting to the baby, as he might have babbled a lullaby into her ear.

Then the snow fell.

At first I thought it was more ash. Flakes from the flames. But one of the boys in the huddle near us whooped. '*Snow!*' Everyone in the crowd seemed to pirouette, following the flakes around them, amazed at the incongruity of the night.

Even Prins turned away from the fire to look at me. 'Snow?' his face drifted apart as though he was drunk. 'Snow?'

○

We walked back towards my house letting the snowflakes settle on us. Prins looked greyer in the head, darker in the face. Going down to my house we seemed to enter a whirlpool where the snow was flying in every direction. The street lights seemed to draw the flakes to them, like moths to a burning prayer. Prins kept grinning and saying, 'Snow,' as if he was naming it for the first time. Garden walls, and the leaves of my neighbour's evergreen shrubs in the front garden, were turning fuzzy with this quietly grow-ing whiteness. The sound level of the whole neighbourhood had dropped. When Prins spoke it sounded as if he was enclosed by a net of frozen water.

'It'll make their job easier,' he said.

'Whose?'

'The firemen. This snow will dampen the fire, no?'

I said I didn't know. The fire seemed such a furnace I thought the snow would be burnt off before it got anywhere close. Evaporating two hundred feet up in the boiling smoke. 'It won't even get near,' I said.

'You mean the hot air will shrug it off. The clouds roll away, huh?'

'Something like that.'

The house was dark. I unlocked my three mortise locks and went in first to turn on the lights.

'I never thought of it before,' Prins mused when we got inside, 'but you know that hedge I told you Sunderam, our old gardener, got so worked up about? How he was crying recalling how *Amma* told him to cut it down?'

I turned up the thermostat in the hall: nineteen to twenty-two centigrade, and turned off the answering machine.

'Well I *remember* that.' Prins had narrowed his eyes as if to concentrate on my answering machine. '*I remember a fire*. I never realized until now that it must have been that same hedge, you know. The one that Sunderam was so weepy about. It must have been the burning of that. A terrific fire. Not like this one. Only a bonfire, I guess, but for me it was huge. I could stand right up next to the crackling and spitting monster. It was wonderful. A dragon burning bright.'

His eyes were, too.

'Tea? coffee? Milky coffee to warm up?' I asked.

'Yes, please,' he answered, as if speaking to somebody

else, before turning back to me with his story about the burning bush. 'We must have been burning this huge mountain of stuff in a fantastic bonfire in the garden. All the smoke and ash and everything would have gone straight into the next-door house.'

'Bellevue?'

'Esra must have thought we were trying to smoke him out.'

'Were you?'

'I wonder. D'you think that was what the old girl was up to? Or maybe it was my father trying to get at him? With *Amma* helping him. Is that possible? The good man biting back. But smoking someone out, that sounds more like Esra's style, you know.'

'Taste of his own medicine?' I remembered Pearl talking about Esra lighting a ring of fire around Arcadia in an effort to rid his ancestral land of intruders.

Prins laughed. 'Could be. Could be.'

I went into the kitchen and lit the gas ring for the milk pan. The flame was pristine blue and piped out in neat shapes; all merging into an invisible centre which, like Prins's imagination, only manifested itself through another surface later, a long time later, through the bubbling of the milk.

Prins followed me. 'I thought the hedge was a kind of test bed, you know. Maybe my father had it planted. Or maybe Esra had it planted. Somehow it was not hers, you know. That is why she had to kamikaze it. Making everything so dark. But I never imagined that maybe they burned it down just to fire up old man Esra, fuming next door.' Prins laughed again. 'That's great. Just her, you know. I bet it was her idea.'

'It would only irritate him though, wouldn't it? Wouldn't that cause more problems?'

'So?' Prins beamed. 'Irritate the old goat. What better fun?'

Outside the snow had become heavier. It fell steadily, gaining more direction: downward. It was beginning to settle on the window sill and along the fence, which was illuminated by the kitchen lights. The whiteness was ghostly. Still tentative. You could see darkness between the flakes. Even the thin layers that lined the surfaces seemed to be slightly opaque with darkness, blackness, behind or underneath. It looked unreal. Temporary.

VII

TWILIGHT

I took the coffee and went into my sitting room, a paler, unfinished reflection of Pearl's. I drew the curtains and turned on the table lamps. A few minutes later Prins, who had gone upstairs while I poured the coffee, reappeared. 'The verdict,' Prins pronounced, 'was accidental death.' I started to laugh, thinking it was one of his lavatorial jokes, then realized he was talking about his father.

Jason Ducal had died on March 22nd 1956, at eight-fifteen in the evening. He was found on the floor of his office with a bullet in his head, and a smashed watch on his wrist. A radio had been left on, its inner valves incandescent. Next door Eddy Kaduwira, Chairman of Sanderson Bros., also lay dead, with the gun that killed both of them in his hand.

Prins was holding a black notebook and a plastic wallet

with copies of the early newspaper reports of the incident, the death certificate, and the coroner's report. He had brought them hidden in his small shoulder-bag. The picture that emerged from the official papers was so consistent, Prins declared, that he felt he had been there. 'More than been there, you know,' he insisted, 'I feel I have seen the movie. I know the story from all the angles, because every cock-arsed theory fits so perfectly. Like cogs linking one wheel to another and everything turns in turn.' He spread the documents on my pine table like an expert croupier. The newspaper articles included a studio portrait of Jason and the Chairman, Eddy Kaduwira, a corpulent, moustachioed man. Jason looked different from the only other photo of him I had seen: the one with Pearl in 1938. The newspaper picture showed a somewhat portly, altogether more serious face. I was intrigued. 'Do you have any pictures of the Vatunases as well?' I wanted to compare portraits.

Prins looked taken aback. 'No.' Then he sighed, 'Not even Lola's.'

We examined his neat dossier that night, and every time I go over it in my mind, I see more of what Prins must have seen then . . .

His dark, blotchy photocopy of the front page of that day's newspaper was full of preposterous deaths: 'Mango led to boy's death' . . . 'Killer-gun found in Hanwell house' . . . 'The wrong man murdered at petrol station.'

'The day – March 22nd 1956 – is stiflingly hot,' Prins began. 'At Sanderson Bros., the monthly Board meeting finishes early because the heat is too much to stay in the room for longer than an hour. The Chairman, Eddy Kaduwira, claps his hands loudly at the end of the hour, "Good show, chaps. Let us meet again next week for a second innings. How's that? I think we deserve a bit of a break today." They take the rest of the afternoon off. All except one Jason Ducal who is in considerable agitation. The Board meeting had not discussed the Budego issue which was the single most important item on the agenda. "We will make it an early morning meeting, Jason. Before the heat is up, eh?" Eddy strokes his silver moustache with one hand, hiding a small smile. The other stays stuck as always, deep in his trouser pocket. My father, Jason, is fuming. "Chanmi," he calls out to one of his colleagues. "You didn't say anything." Chanmi lowers his head, his eyebrows sweeping back, "What to do? With all this Jayanti talk and *poya*-bans, this may not be the best time for your Lankan usquebaugh." He looks up, "See you at Pigalle tomorrow night? Jam-session, yes? Pukka jazz."'

The Board comprised six members plus the Chairman and Jason. Two of the members were particularly garrulous with the press in the days that followed, and their observations and comments on the behaviour of both Eddy Kaduwira and Jason are quoted everywhere in the newspaper articles Prins showed me.

Jason did not go home that day. He spent another hour, at least, getting his assistant to bring all the papers they had on the Budego venture to his office. Then, at a quarter past five in the afternoon, after the junior staff had finished their day's work, Jason had called Dr Denzil Fernando. This conversation was reported in the press.

Dr Denzil Fernando was a Doctor of Philosophy from an obscure American university; he had a passion for the paranormal and an interest in psychology. He had set himself up as a consultant and provided services to the wealthier sections of Colombo society. Prins claimed that people assumed from his title that he was a physician, and came to him for treatment; he would treat them, explaining to those who questioned him that ninety per cent of medical ailments were psychosomatic and therefore he could help his patients as well as any GP; others apparently came for business advice, marriage counselling, sexual guidance and even legal advice. Prins laughed and said that Denzil treated them all as clients in search of therapy and seemed to satisfy some need that they sometimes did not even know they had. He had the knack of flattering them until they felt better. 'He was a charmist, licensed to lie,' Prins said. Jason had got to know him when he started playing golf, hooking to the left at every hole.

One article reported that Jason had complained to Denzil about the impossibility of getting the Chairman to take a decision, and of Eddy's predilection to go off in the afternoon to his beach-side playroom. 'Every time that Mr Ducal had prepared the ground, Eddy Kaduwira had shied away. "He shouldn't be in this position. We can't wait another week," Jason had cried in exasperation,' according to Dr Denzil.

'Eddy Kaduwira himself was on the verge of a break-down,' Denzil Fernando was also quoted as saying in another article. 'His life was degenerating and therefore on this day he made a supreme effort to assert his will over life: and he did this by taking his own life. A classic case, psychologically speaking. But with tragic consequences for Mr Jason Ducal.'

But the immediate reports made clear that what pushed Eddy to fire the gun was not the oscillating fortunes of the local liquor trade; rather, it was the exposure of his sexual predilections in a police raid that took place on the afternoon of the same day.

After the curtailment of the Board meeting Eddy had rushed down the coast to where he had set up a secret nesting place for young fisher-boys, the 'beach-side playroom' that Jason had referred to. But shortly after he had arrived the police, led by a fervent young Inspector Cooray, had burst into the mat-and-tat rattan room expecting to arrest two Scandinavian seamen on charges of lewd assault. Finding the famously moustachioed pillar

of Cinnamon Gardens commerce floundering in the ropes
of a hammock sock-full of nude pubescent boys was a
tremendous shock to Inspector Cooray, who happened to
be a distant relative of Eddy Kaduwira. 'The whole thing
might have been quietly swept under a prickly straw mat,'
Prins pointed at a grey grainy photo of a rotund bare-
bodied man with his hands in front of his face, 'but for the
fact that a journalist with a camera had been dragooned
by the cops, desperate to improve their public image.'
They needed a fillip after Operation Ganja; some success
in at least combating the spread of insidious foreign
debauchery daily bemoaned by the nation's readers. It was
an auspicious year for political platforms for all sections of
society.

'Have a look at this,' Prins unfolded a centre spread.
Eddy Kaduwira, encapsulated in 48-point capitals as
EDDY-BEDDY, shown in a series of resuscitated photographs commemorating his many achievements as the
businessman of yesterday; slapping the backs and shaking
the hands of the great and the good of a gracious and fine
post-colonial society: Ambassadors, Ministers and even
Prime Ministers. According to the lead article Eddy-Beddy
was allowed to drive home to his unsuspecting family
while the young Inspector Cooray consulted with his
superiors on how he should treat this delicate situation.

'On the road, somewhere between a church and a

temple, Eddy Kaduwira saw the shape of his life very clearly,' Denzil Fernando gleefully conjectured as a celebrity sleuth. 'He stopped by the infamous shrine of Srijan and contemplated the wretchedness of his wastrel life. There he would have seen the way to act decisively and cut the knots that had embroiled him in indecisiveness and degeneracy. A kind of spiritual enlightenment in that unusual place.'

The early reports simply noted the bizarre double deaths and Jason's demise; they dwelt much more on Eddy Kaduwira's sensational, utterly reprehensible sexual habits. But the later reports, after the inquest, told a neater story of suicide and tragic misfortune. Instead of going home Eddy had driven himself, unescorted, to the Sanderson Bros. building. He had marched into his office and sat behind his Chairman's desk as if to survey his life's work. Then he had apparently pulled out a World War II Mauser automatic from his desk drawer, put it in his mouth and pulled the trigger. The bullet had gone through his mouth, severing his brainstem, and passed clean out of the back of his neck. The bullet not only instantly killed Eddy Kaduwira, but burst through the glazed teak panels of his economically partitioned office and unerringly smashed into Jason Ducal's skull. It killed him on the spot as he stood listening to the special Radio Ceylon anniversary broadcast commemorating the father of the nation, the country's first

Prime Minister, who had died four years earlier when he fell off a horse.

'This is the official account,' Prins shook the paper in my face. 'Can you believe it? No wonder the goons today think they can get away with anything. As if my father would have put his ear to the wall to collect a bloody bullet in it at eight-fifteen in the evening.'

With the cull of the Chairman and his go-ahead Deputy, Sanderson Bros. withdrew from the Budego affair and began its slow descent into eventual bankruptcy. 'It's so neat,' Prins clenched his fist, 'so bloody convenient.' He was convinced an assassin had murdered them both, separately. Homicide was on the rise all over the country, Prins claimed. Everybody wanted to analyse the social phenomenon, but nobody seemed to be very keen to investigate what Prins saw as a double crime.

Jason Ducal's funeral was attended by an enormous crowd from the commercial sector, the Golf Club and the residential district dominated by the Vatunases. Even Delia Vatunas, with Sita in tow, had visited Pearl to pay their respects, but Esra and Tivoli had not stepped into Arcadia. Only in Bellevue did the ubiquitous white flag of mourning flutter a little wanly.

Then, within three weeks, Mohan Jayasuriya had given up journalism and the *Daily Watch* had exposed the hoax about Budego's liquor; Jason was vindicated. But without him Sanderson Bros. was unable to act. Esra Vatunas took over Ambrose Budego & Son, and Jason Ducal became a figure of minor tragedy among his contemporaries.

o

From what Prins had told me, and from what I have learned since then, I could see how Esra Vatunas had always thrived on uncertainty and the misfortune of others. That year with its manic electioneering, communal posturing and leaps of aggression, he had plenty of opportunity to live off both. By all accounts he was doing extremely well.

With Ambrose Budego & Son under his control, Esra began his experiments blending the fresh May toddy tap with the old Budego vats. He switched his own tipple to the Budego family's reserve stock of double-distilled de luxe arrack, which also became the only drink served to anyone who visited Bellevue. He was reported in the press as being 'in good spirits' despite the clamour of a rush of opportunistic teetotallers. As Prins put it: 'His son was ensconced in a family of his own three hundred yards away, his grand-children were growing with considerably more spunk than the wayward Tivoli had shown, and his business empire had become as powerful as the roots of a Koswatte bitter-weed.'

Political ferment and the controversy over the demon drink in the country simply provided a little lift for him.

Although he liked to gloat in private, Esra tried to repress this urge when in public. And as his businesses sprouted in unexpected sectors he was inevitably drawn out into the public eye more than he had originally wished. 'At his own table with guests, toadies and grog-urchins present he would sneer at the failures of his contemporaries and the foolhardiness of his competitors, but at the invariable gala openings he would have to attend he would keep his jaws clenched until his tiny teeth began to wear thin.'

'Was Delia oblivious of her husband's sharpening profile?' I asked.

'Delia kept the domestic situation under perfect control and provided him with much-needed social graces. She didn't seem to notice how, unlike other successful men, he grew thinner and bonier and sharper each day. It was as if he was reducing himself to a pair of barely honed jaws capable of tearing anything and everything to pieces. But Delia saw only his growing ambitions and incomprehensible achievements: the openings, the launchings, the investitures. A shining, glowing bubble floating higher and higher.

'At the age of sixty-six, Esra Vatunas was a hugely successful survivor. Nothing could stop him from achieving his grandest commercial ambitions. But he was beginning to develop a new ambition; he seemed to want a different kind of recognition, the recognition that his father, Buttons, had had as a man whose life and achievements were seen, rightly or wrongly, to have been of benefit to more than himself. He wanted to feel that not only did he have power over others because of their ignorance, but power over them because of their loyalty to him. He wanted a constituency, and to be recognized by that constituency as their leader, their spokesman. He told Delia that when he died he wanted all the roads from Bellevue to Kanatta decked in white, and have every church, vihara, mosque and synagogue buzzing with prayer for him. *Buzzing*.' Prins chuckled.

'It was probably only then that Esra began to feel that death might cheat him out of his rightful honours; that the crudest politicos of his day, the warped pillar-heads of the Chamber of Commerce and even the pathetic ethical foetuses of this world, like his enemy Jason, might have been more wily than he: their deaths have more mourners, their ends more of a blaze of glory, their funerals be bigger and more stately than his would ever be. And this apparently made him feel sick to his contracted stomach.'

But, unfazed, he then set about redesigning the Vatunas tomb – specifying the hierarchy and final resting place of three generations, and even the lettering on each of his descendants' gravestones – and, at the same time, cultivating high society to regain his father's position in the minds of his fellows. He began to entertain politicians, priests, paper barons at a dining table replete with his new arrack-based elixir – Vambrosia. Through his fancy blue bottle, if not through his dealings in coconut oil, he intended to win the stupefied minds as well as the envious hearts of all his contemporaries. The patronage of wealth and wine, he claimed, was a classic recipe for success in the world.

'It did work, up to a point,' Prins said. By the end of three years, Vambrosia was on the lips of all the hottest heads of the island. And by the time of his death, another three years later, the swankier de luxe version had slipped down the throats of most of the well-to-do, while a large proportion of the 'ne'er do wells', as Esra had called them, reeled to the kick of the cheaper Vambrose Plain. Within ten years a Vambrosia in some form had become an essential accompaniment to any meeting of indulgent, smarmy minds anywhere on the island and Esra Vatunas was known as the man who had been behind the taste of the times. The patron saint of all God's drunks and dreamers. And no one talked of prohibition ever again.

o

'Esra's greatest *political* triumph of the year was when he enticed two opposing Members of Parliament to Bellevue

and got them paralytic on his new prototype Vambrosia.'
Prins said that this was a story that had been going around
Colombo's drinking circles for a long time.

Esra had noticed that two senior MPs in particular were
very partial to hard liquor. One of them, Pucksy Mendis,
was a man of large proportions and well-known indul-
gences; the other, Fosil Gunasena, was a businessman
turned politician. Esra invited them to his house one night
to meet an investor from Zurich – Alexis – who had tar-
geted the island for his mid-1950s portfolio. He had also
asked a senior civil servant to sit in at the meeting. 'A man
who didn't open his mouth in front of Esra, but couldn't
keep it shut afterwards.'

Both Pucksy Mendis and Fosil Gunasena had arrived
before the investor. They were finding the new mood of
abstemiousness among their colleagues difficult to cope
with, and took every opportunity to counter it, at least
within their own bodies. Esra met them on his veranda
with two large special-blend drinks in his hands. They
shook hands by passing the glasses across. 'Come, sit down,
have a drink,' he had commanded.

'The front veranda of Bellevue has a brown floor polished like marble,' Prins described it like a filmset. 'Coconut
flowers festooned the entrance to the inner rooms like
sharks' teeth in a gigantic jaw. Weird alembic vases. Pucksy
Mendis sat back in one of the vast fussy cane chairs and

shook his leg in a non-stop tremble. The ice rattled in his glass. "So, who is this Swiss fellow you want us to meet then?" Pucksy Mendis asked Esra.'

Esra had met Alexis at a cocktail party that the British High Commissioner had given. He explained that Alexis represented the milk-and-military industries of Europe, and was interested in the surplus labour of the coastal strip.

'What we need,' Pucksy Mendis had said, 'is *money* for our development, not cowbells.'

'Have another drink, young man. How can you have any development without a proper drink?' Esra had retorted.

'I say, the PM should hear that.' Fosil Gunasena had become very agitated. 'All the bloody parties are dry now. Helluva bloody joke – this man-made drought.'

By the time Alexis arrived Pucksy Mendis and Fosil Gunasena were distinctly tipsy. The visitor was delighted to find the two well-known parliamentarians in such a malleable mood, and a distinguished man between them that he knew he could do business with.

That evening Pucksy Mendis and Fosil Gunasena drank almost two bottles of the new Vambrosia and were completely captivated by Alexis's vision of rearming the ceremonial troops of the nation, and vitalizing the burgeoning population of the south through rapid industrial growth in munitions manufacturing. 'All financed through soft loans,' he had said *sotto voce*. 'Let the Americans play with free milk powder, but you people need to grow up now. They'll never give you atomic power until you show you can fight like a Corregidor veteran.'

'By nine o'clock both MPs were dead drunk. Pucksy was rolling from side to side as though he was on the high seas, and Fosil was giggling like a pissed newt.' Prins threw back his head and laughed. 'When the call came for an emergency meeting by their two rival top-dog politicos later that evening, it was impossible for them to go.' Esra helped them concoct their excuses and thereby clasped their political future securely in his hand forever.

o

'But before he found his two rooks to play with, Esra had gained a bishop of sorts: Srijan, our infamous maverick monk.' Prins looked at me, waiting for a sign of surprise. Srijan was an unorthodox renegade but nevertheless, in the kingdom of free faiths, a self-proclaimed monk of some standing.

Prins described him as extraordinarily hairless; the hairlessness seemed congenital, and not the result of obsessive shaving as in the case of the more muscular, saffron-clad orders of the land. His robes seemed like the petals of a flower from which his face bloomed, with lips that promised a well of wisdom and exquisite poetry. His flesh was as smooth as crystal glass but his presence was said to have been breathtakingly sensual. He was quite unlike any other monk, or mendicant, known in the district or outside it. He had appeared from nowhere and taken refuge in a ruined temple, a few miles south of town, which had been abandoned for decades. There he spent his days practising the art of calligraphy, writing out aphoristic notices in several different scripts – Sinhala, Tamil, English, Chinese, Arabic – and posting them around the grounds. He extended an aura of wisdom and sanctity which protected him and gave the blighted local community some sense of beneficence. But he was an unknown monk; tolerated by the orthodox on the assumption that he was harmless, and provided some small flame of enlightenment in a dismal part of the country where only brothels and taverns had ever provided any kind of illumination, except in the dim, distant dark ages.

Srijan rocketed to national prominence when he started writing to the newspapers disputing the conjectures of Dr Denzil Fernando. Not only did he dispute the suggestion that Eddy-Beddy Kaduwira might have come to a conclusion about his need for suicide outside Srijan's place, as though it was some convoluted and confused Pauline revelation, but he did so with evident and unmonkly relish and, in the English newspapers, he wrote in highly suspect rhyming couplets:

> Dear Sir,
> Doctor Fernando is completely wrong,
> his shot is wide and ridiculously long.
> Eddy-Beddy was not going to Damascus,
> he and this shrine had nothing to discuss.
> To be enlightened is not to be dead,
> nor to put a bullet in your head.

The newspaper editors loved it. In years to come mad monks would overwhelm all their front pages with murder and intrigue, but Srijan was the first to make the headlines: 'RHYMING SRI SLUGS DR DENZY'. He became a celebrity. He was interviewed by the Sunday papers and found to understand half a dozen languages. He could recite Dante and Tagore in their original tongues and, in English, could speak in verse: erudition that seemed not only unfashionably perverse, but deeply unpatriotic as well. The radio asked him to talk to a nation hysterical about the jumble of language in a culture of purity, and he broadcast a stream of mellifluous morphemes the likes of which had never been heard before on the island's airwaves. But he was always evasive about his own past:

TWILIGHT

The past is a figment of your imagination,
just like the history of any nation.

None of Colombo's teeming journalists and cub
reporters were ever able to dig up any information about
Srijan's past, or how he came to be so well-endowed – as a
linguist. There was no school who claimed him, no monk
who had tutored him, no religious order willing to accept
him, no family that could demonstrate kinship. Only
rumours: that he was a Russian émigré linked to Madame
Blavatsky, that he was the unacknowledged offspring of a
Kandyan chief, or even the eccentric bastard of an English
Governor. He had a fast-growing following of ordinary
folk who believed that he was the only light in the darkness
of their lives. His odd erudition and mysterious past simply
confirmed their view of him as an extraordinary and gracious presence sent to calm their troubled and turbulent
times. At the very least he was a wonderful diversion to a
nation harangued by overbearing politicians spoiling for a
fight. People came to his temple from all around to read his
latest notices, posted like the lines of a fragmentary poem
created from a medley of languages. Intricate aphorisms in
Arabic one way and English the other: 'Life is but a preparation for death.' Ideogram editorials with one-line
subtitles: 'Trust the voice not the tongue.' And political
commentaries invoking honey pots and Winnie-the-Pooh.

Esra had discovered Srijan much earlier than the rest of the nation. He was keen on developing local allies and as Srijan was an influential figure in the neighbourhood of the Budego distillery, he invited him to lunch at Bellevue early in his campaign.

Esra received the reply by return:

> Luncheon at your residence would be divine,
> in more ways than one, impossible to decline.

The event was an entirely private affair. There were no other guests. Delia supervised the quietly sumptuous meal in keeping with the monkly requirements of health, inner wealth and vitality. Luncheon was served in the huge Bellevue dining room, with the two of them at one end of the grand dining table produced to the Bacchanalian design of Esra's father, Buttons Vatunas. The table was made out of the remains of an old Dutch staircase from a Hultsdorf villa, and had rococo grapes and roses springing out of its balustrade legs like the genitalia of a troop of tumescent pleasure-seekers.

'Srijan did not belong to any orthodox structure: Buddhist, Hindu, Muslim, Jewish or Christian, and Esra did not know what made him tick. What did this creature want most out of life: books? alcohol? sex? Cadbury's? Esra needed the facts before he could capture his spirit.'

Prins showed me a copy of a verse written by Srijan, his
version of this encounter:

> There came to me an invitation out of the blue,
> it had the scent of a man who loved a coup.
> At his grand bucolic table
> I told him my favourite little fable:
> there was a monk who wanted freedom so much
> that he found there was nothing he could ever touch.
> In the end he felt he was locked in a cage
> like a word never read but trapped in a page.
> My host, in turn, opened a bottle of booze,
> I said I was not in a position to choose.

o

Prins had found it in a book of doggerel by Srijan on Lola's
bookshelf.

'You read this stuff?' he had asked her.

She told him that it was the only book of verse that her
grandfather – Esra Vatunas – had ever owned. Prins had
come across Srijan's couplets in the correspondence
columns of the newspapers of 1956, but had not considered it of any real significance. Srijan had been concerned

about Eddy Kaduwira and his spiritual condition but had not mentioned Jason in any of his candied verse. However, the reference to the Vatunas table and booze in the book drew Prins into thinking more about Srijan and what he might know about Jason's death, rather than Eddy-Beddy's dissipation.

Srijan was still alive at the time, living in a modernized bungalow in the grounds of the old temple. It was off the main coast road and a little way from the sea. Prins said he could imagine that Eddy Kaduwira might have slipped past the place taking a short cut home – or if he was heading for the Sanderson Bros. head office. The bungalow had been renovated by a benefactor. Even the temple had been restored in parts.

'He seemed to live more like a don than a *bhikku*,' Prins told me. 'The house was comfortable, much bigger than I expected. Quite fancy furniture. He had a pukka desk by the window. Looking straight at the temple trees.'

Srijan would have been in his sixties when Prins met him, but Prins was impressed by his youthful looks. He had no hair to go grey, nothing to recede or disappear. His eyes were clear, his skin supple, his hands firm and full.

Prins had heard that Srijan observed surgery hours. He was apparently always there in the bungalow but would receive visitors and talk only after four in the afternoon. It was customary to take him food to eat.

Prins had arrived with a bunch of bananas. 'I got those nice small ones,' he said. He had come quarter of an hour early, in case there might be other visitors. As always, Prins had wanted to be first and take the lion's share. But that day nobody else was there. Prins had sat on a bench on the veranda in full view of Srijan who was at his desk by the window writing, but he had not been acknowledged. Prins said that Srijan had seemed to stare right through him at the ruins that lay beyond the garden. Small notices with Srijan's latest epigrams had been dotted about, each with its own small oil lamp at the ready, making the outline of a great wheel of life. 'The one nearest to me was elaborately decorated: "To wait a while is the best we can hope to do in this life."' Then at four o'clock sharp Srijan had risen from his desk and come out onto the veranda, smiling beatifically, to greet him as if he had just arrived.

Prins had placed his bunch of bananas on the small wooden table and the monk had nodded graciously. Prins, for once, had been lost for words. He had not known where to begin: a cross-examination? a plea for wisdom? solace? forensic evidence?

Eventually Srijan had quoted a line of Shakespeare at him: 'all our yesterdays have lighted fools . . .'

Prins had jumped. 'What?'

'You want to speak English, like our Shakis Perera? You

are on a quest. In search of what is no longer there. So you need sustenance like I need bananas.' Srijan had laughed, peeling the soft, red skin in half-inch strips.

'Your Reverend, you remember a Mr Esra Vatunas?'

Srijan had laughed again, 'But of course. The man who wanted to be a king, Mr Ducal.'

Prins, startled, had asked how he knew his name.

'From your business card. There, in your hand, waiting to be passed to me.'

Prins had handed him his card sheepishly. He had explained how he had noticed that many years ago Srijan had come into public prominence when he started to write to the newspapers about Eddy Kaduwira.

'But you would have been just a baba, then.'

'Yes, but I was looking into the Kaduwira business recently.'

'"Eddy-Beddy, the man with a penchant for pricks," that's what this Srijan said,' but Prins had kept a straight face. He had asked whether Srijan knew anything of his father, Jason.

'Poor Jason Ducal. Yes,' Srijan had said. 'I knew of him. A good man, I think, in this world of impossible desires.'

'But you never met him?' Prins had asked.

'Bugger was so evasive. A real politician, you know,' Prins clucked. 'He sat there eating my plantains and thinking of something clever to say. In the end he said, "We have all met at one time or another, in one life or another. We meet again and again. That is the way the wheel turns. It is nothing and yet it is everything." As if that answered my bloody question.'

O

But Srijan had met Jason, in the ordinary sense, at least once. He told Prins about it only after Prins had visited him again. 'I had to go again,' Prins said. 'You know, something drew me there like a fish-hook's prick.'

At the appointed time, Srijan had come out and beamed: his teeth, his cheeks, his pate gleamed as if he was in rapture. Prins had repeated the question about his father.

'You have his perseverance, even if not his appearance,' Srijan had replied. 'Your father was a good man but, despite his worldly success, he was sometimes a little reckless. He'd rush and go too fast, often misunderstand what others said.'

Prins had kept his mouth shut and his ears open. 'Yes,' Srijan had admitted, 'Jason Ducal came here. He needed some place just to sit and think. You see, nothing ever happens here; you can wait forever. Eventually everything will become clear. If that is what you desire.'

O

The final item Prins uncovered that night in my sitting room was a photograph of a small pen and ink drawing done by Tivoli: the back view of a woman reading a book. A background of wild foliage is hinted at by dark and gloomy scrolls that weave in and out of its pages. The woman's hair is undone. She is sitting on a garden bench with one of her legs folded under her. In a corner a 'T' – his signature. 'Burnt umber,' Prins stated, 'dated 22.3.56.' Prins had seen it in Lola's room and was struck by the date. He had told her, just as he told me, 'It is the very same day that my father was killed.'

Things seem to always fall into a pattern, especially for someone like Prins. The more he looks, the more it conforms.

VIII

DARKNESS

'It's all there,' Prins pushed the clippings towards me and slumped back in my threadbare sofa. 'You can imagine what it was like, but I don't know why the rest of us were not there. My mother took us away from the house. Why?'

We had the TV on in my sitting room as Pearl would have done, with subtitles crackling out of its fractured circuits: a failing tube. I switched channels and found a Gene Kelly retrospective on BBC2.

I remembered watching *Singin' in the Rain* with Pearl once. When the credits rolled at the end, she knocked back the last of her sherry, 'You see clearly only when it is empty, no? You can't look back until it is, but by then it's over. Empty. Gone. You have to turn yourself upside down and start all over again.' She looked moody.

'When did you first see this film?' I asked. *Singin' in the Rain* was one of her regulars; she would be quite elated with the song and dance but at the end she never seemed very happy.

She looked at me as if she was trying to decide something. She spoke more slowly than usual. 'The first time was the night before Jason died. It was a terrible time, we were not getting on at all . . . The atmosphere was so stultifying, you know, that I even arranged for all the children to go to my outstation aunty. He didn't like that either. But we needed to sort so much out. I didn't know how. I needed something to cheer me up. My friend Ishrani was the one who suggested we go watch a film. Ishrani is Mira's mother, you know. Really tall and wears a lot of gold all the time. Enormous armful of gold bangles, and always gold around her neck, on her nose. Too much for me.' Pearl rubbed the cat's-eye silver ring she always wore. 'I prefer silver myself, but she was mad about gold. She loved dressing up – like Mira, you know. Lovely bright saris and always decorated by at least one gold thread. Sometimes, a big border of gold brocade. But even with all that metal, she always brought some light and air wherever she went. Must be that laugh she had. I'll never forget that.' Pearl heaved herself up and went over to a small cabinet under the TV set. She opened it and pulled out another bottle of sherry. 'I didn't even know what was on, but I remember Ishrani said, "*The Seven Year Itch* or *Gone With the Wind*." I could do without the seven-year nonsense . . . Here, open this, Chip *putha*.' She passed me the bottle.

'So we went. Ishrani parked her car – a tiny Fiat she could barely squeeze into – at the car park at the Majestic and started laughing. Shoulders rolling and getting bigger, swelling like something was going to burst inside her. "Why?" I asked "Why so hysterical?" "The film," she giggled, "*Gone With the Wind* is gone away." There was a notice about the film being cancelled. They had *Singin' in the Rain* as a special instead. "Never mind," she said, "it'll do the trick." "What trick?" I asked. "The trick of cheering a sourpuss up."

'She had to wriggle out of her car. Her husband, such a big-shot judge, always wanted to get her a new car. He told her that she was too big for her Fiat. Ishrani would get furious. "Why, what are you trying to say? You calling me fat now?" He would say, "No, it is just that your car is a baby car. It is too small." She would then hit the roof: "Millions of Italians go in these." She knew that her husband was a great fan of Sophia Loren; he would only go to see a film if it starred Sophia Loren. Ishrani liked to think she was *our* Sophia Loren; she was sure that Sophia Loren had stepped out of a Fiat just like hers in some film or the other. Every time she got out of her car, she imagined the scene in the film. And each time she would ask me whether what she needed to do was change her sari for a skirt. She'd ask, "Would you ever wear one?" I'd say I would change a baby Fiat for one of those new Studebakers any day, if Jason offered. Anyway, I told her, Sophia Loren is now wearing a sari in Roma. It was big news: she was getting ready to come to Colombo for the filming of *Elephant Bill*. Ishrani got into a real state although I was much more excited about our *Rekawa* that was being done around about the same time.'

'Did it work?' I asked. 'Did the dancing cheer you up?'

'I love watching a man dance. Gene Kelly is no Fred Astaire, but he is athletic. Jason didn't like dancing, you know. He moved so woodenly on the floor. He'd be the broom. He was happiest when he could sit down and order the food and drink. Giving orders, making rules, he liked that sort of thing. Following somebody else's invisible pattern was not for him. Even his golf, you know, was a little eccentric.'

o

For the last three days of his life, Jason had concentrated almost wholly on the job of securing the distillery he had identified as the business of the future, as had Esra Vatunas and his son Tivoli next door.

But the week had started badly for him. Pearl told me how she had asked him whether he would be free to go out on Wednesday evening.

'I can't,' He had been extremely brusque. 'There is this meeting on Thursday and I have to get everything sorted out.'

It was their wedding anniversary but he had forgotten.

'But you have all day,' Pearl held out her hand, re-enacting the scene.

'On Wednesday afternoon I have to play golf.'

'*Golf*? Have to?'

'I arranged to play with Chanmi. It's the only chance I'll get to talk to him before the meeting. I need the evening free.'

'Will you have *any time* for me this week?'

'I'm sorry.' His face had sagged. He had pulled his feet together in contrition, or perhaps to draw strength from the ground under his soles. The earth below the floor. The breathless rage at the centre of the world.

'I'll call Ishrani then,' Pearl had shrugged. 'If you can't come, you can't. I'll go somewhere with her.'

'Yes, you go. Please. I'm sorry but this week is hell.'

'It was such an impossible situation,' Pearl seemed to buckle under the tension of the scene she recalled.

'You should take things slower. What is this mad rush all the time,' she had said.

'It's business, my dear.'

'Business? Jason, you do not understand the first thing about business.'

Jason's face changes shape as his thoughts ricochet around his head, pulling and pinching his skin, releasing a disconnected smile.

'What?'

'You are not a businessman. You like playing these games, but doing business is not going crazy like you are. What you are doing with all this rushing around and madness is what losers who are going out of business do.'

Jason stares at Pearl as though he had never seen her speak before. His face ceased its agitation.

'You've been successful Jason, but you don't seem to have learned why you have been successful. And if you are not careful, you will lose it all. I can see that.'

'How?'

'You'll lose it because you don't seem to know what you have. You won't even know when it goes, until it is too late.'

'What? What are you talking about?'

'Just stop everything for a while, Jason. Stop and look around you. Look at me, for God's sake.'

'I will. I will. But I can't go to the cinema this week. You

have to understand. This week I have got to get this deal
sorted out. After that I will take it easy. I promise.
Everything will be much better.'

O

Jason and Pearl had been married for twenty years. He
must have been stunned when, after all that time, his wife
suddenly told him that his whole career was mismanaged.
Flawed from the beginning.

I never divulged to Prins what I thought had happened.
The sourness of those last few days that Pearl talked about.
I let his question about why she moved them out of Arcadia
hang between us and melt in the glare of a succession of
show-time movie clips. Prins was breathing heavily; his
upper lids slid halfway down his eyes like cowls. I suggested
he go upstairs to bed.

'No,' he protested. 'The only way to handle the jet lag is
to keep trucking until the normal bedtime of wherever you
are.' But he looked exhausted. 'Flying in this direction
should be easy,' he added with a frown.

After about a minute of silence, he gave in. 'But maybe
I'll just go stretch out for a bit.' He got up quickly and
hurried out of the room.

Pearl is sitting in a wicker chair by the gramophone. Jason is opposite her.

'Do you want a drink?'

She refuses.

'Lemonade? Ginger beer?'

Pearl says no. 'No, no, no.'

He looks around. 'I think I need a beer.'

'It's Jinasena's night off.'

'I know, I know,' Jason retorts. 'I'll get it.'

He goes to the back of the house, to the refrigerator between the dining room and the kitchen. He finds a bottle of beer and opens it with the bottle opener tied to the door handle of the Electrolux. He picks up a glass from the teak cabinet and pours himself the beer.

'It's been twenty years, you know,' he lifts the glass at Pearl. 'Twenty years we have been married.'

She nods but says nothing. She looks at him as if she was trying to work out what is going on inside his head. It's too late now, too late to remember, to celebrate. She didn't think he realized, even then, about the anniversary.

'You remember the first years?' he asks.

'Before we came here?'

'Yes, but all those years, you know?'

'What are you thinking of?'

'I was thinking, why has it taken twenty years for you to

tell me what you told me today?'

'About what?'

'About getting involved in business. Like you think I am a fool or something.'

'I didn't say you were a fool.'

'You said I didn't know what I was doing. That I was acting like a failure. Isn't that what you said?'

Pearl sighs and turns away.

'You did.' Jason insists. 'You said that successful people, I guess like your father, knew how to behave. I suppose they were more conscientious. Is that it? But what about that trip to England? What about the easy times you had? We had.'

'All I said was that you were getting too busy.'

'Too frantic.'

'Yes, too frantic. You don't need to.'

'You think I don't need to do anything. You think it will all just roll along happily. But I can tell you, it doesn't all just happen automatically. Someone has got to put their shoulder to it. Someone's got to work to keep the show on the road. And it is not just someone, it's me. I have to. Nobody else will. Your father had it easy. He had sick people to deal with, grateful people.'

He tilts his glass, gulps the beer.

Pearl says nothing. Nothing for minutes. Finally she blurts out: 'Do you know what Wednesday is?'

But Pearl's words have a hollowness to them. She is speaking in a house that is empty. For a moment it seems as though they are back in the past of twenty years earlier, when it was just the two of them in a room that had nothing in it, in a town that had nothing of their two entwined lives in it, in a country that lay sleeping, waiting for the earth to heave and break into their dreams.

o

Jason and Pearl slept in the same room but in separate beds. She said, 'He liked a hard bed, but for me I can't sleep if it isn't as soft as a cloud.' On each of the last three nights of his life Jason had slept badly. He kept waking up, startled by a dream about an argument or some kind of conflict.

He wrote copiously, recording every move he made, each morning and each evening of that final week, in the last of the sad blue timebenders that survived him and survived Pearl to fetch up on the shores of my own rapidly degrading life. It seems as though he felt that only by writing it all down in his school-ruled notebook could he keep control of a life in danger of going awry. It is all that remains of that extraordinary week, but it is enough to give me a glimpse and allow me, now, to reconstruct something of those last few days as Pearl must have done. Prins never read Jason's words. He held the very same notebook in his hands once, but didn't even know whose writing marked its pages. By then he didn't want to know anything more, he wanted to break the stranglehold of the past. But even so his father's own words must count for something.

'Have some Ovaltine before sleeping,' Pearl suggested to Jason in an effort at reconciliation.

'You know I can never drink it. The idea of it makes me feel sick.'

'Try it. Soothe your nerves.'

'Next week, it will be different,' Jason was sure.

'So you say, but next week is not in our hands.'

Jason laughed. 'Is it ever?'

Jason laughed for a long time. He could see that she was watching him laugh. She was not laughing. But he didn't stop. *Then it too sounded hollow*, he wrote in blue ink.

○

In his office on Tuesday night Jason mapped out his strategy. He wrote down what he thought needed to be said, and made notes on the Board members who needed to be reassured. For each person he had a list of concerns and a column of points he needed to make to address those concerns. He then went over each point to identify when and how he was going to ensure that this happened and used red ink to star the most important ones.

Chanmi – Stanislaus Chanmugam – a man about ten years his senior, was a major red star. Jason thought he would be the most difficult to convince. Chanmi was a constitutional pessimist. But he was also a bright economist whose opinion could easily sway the others. Fortunately he was also a golfer, and Jason had a plan to use this to his advantage.

Ever since his mentor Iain Stevenson first introduced him to the game, Jason had played golf regularly. According to Pearl, he played to break into the golfing fraternity: the professionals, urbanites, potential politicians practising their cabinet strategies, the new elite. 'He had an insatiable need to belong,' she said, a little dismissively. But, I think, he must have also played because he enjoyed the time it gave him, more or less on his own, to think through his own thoughts. From his journal entries he seemed sometimes intoxicated by his own thoughts, but unable to express them in their full glory to anyone. Hitting a golf ball, watching it define a curve through the air seemed to have released some of the pressure from his head.

A few days earlier he had called Chanmi at his house, 'How about some golf, *men*?'

'When?' Chanmi had answered cautiously.

'Wednesday? Four-thirty? Nine holes?'

There was silence on the line. It was always like that with Chanmi, Jason scrawled in his journal. *He always needed a few seconds before speaking; as he did before choosing a club, or hitting a ball, or puncturing a business proposal.*

'I thought just a quick trot around.'

Chanmi had agreed. It seemed to Jason a good bit of insurance before the Board meeting. *A stroke of genius.* But he must have also thought a walk around a few holes would relax him. *I really need to calm down,* he added.

On the Tuesday night he seemed to have gone over his financial proposal obsessively. There are incomprehensible calculations in the margins of his journal. Nothing quite like this had ever been attempted in the country before. *Buying into the tavern trade, rather than marrying out of it.* But Jason was sure that his economic assumptions made sense. His main worry was that Chanmi's scepticism might dissuade the others. *I need to give him a feeling that this is as much his idea as mine.*

o

On Wednesday afternoon, the day before he died, Jason drives to the Golf Club and parks his Hillman Minx right up against the wall of the clubhouse. He tries to get as much of the car in the shade as possible. His caddie, Tito, appears at the door even before the red dust has settled. He has one edge of his sarong hoisted up and tucked into his waistband. He is a short man, not much taller than Jason's tartan bag of clubs. But he swings the bag onto his shoulder as if it moves on wings. Tito is a brilliant golfer: a scratch player who is better at the game than any of the club members, but who is not allowed to compete in anything but the Caddies Tournament. He is also a spy. Everybody pays him to eavesdrop on the course: the CID, the Government, the Opposition parties, business magnates, even the CIA. He makes up stories for all of them: a born storyteller. But for Jason he has some affection. Tito likes to exchange his golfing tips for tutorials on his correspondence courses. He is constantly taking correspondence courses on politics, history or literature from universities on the other side of the world. He waves a school edition of *Julius Caesar* in front of Jason's face. 'But why sir, did he not beware the Ides of March?'

'Ask me tomorrow, Tito, tomorrow. Is Mr Chanmugam here?'

Tito pushes out his head, chin first, like a tortoise in a tartan shell, indicating the front of the clubhouse.

Jason takes his golf shoes out of the bag and walks over to the clubhouse.

On the veranda of the clubhouse there is room for about a dozen tables for people to sit at and watch golfers play off the first tee and, on the right, approach the ninth green. Further up is the final green: the eighteenth.

Chanmi is sipping lime juice at a table, at the far end, close to a wall that is being repainted.

Jason calls out to him and walks over.

'Very hot,' Chanmi exclaims.

Jason takes note. Is it a complaint? He needs things to start better than this.

'Best place to be on a hot day. Coolest spot this course, they say. Is the lime good?'

Chanmi nods. Jason summons a waiter who is polishing some new brass plates inside the clubhouse.

'Lime juice here as well, please. But quickly. We tee-off in five minutes.'

The waiter hurries away and Jason turns to Chanmi. 'It will cool down soon.'

Chanmi inclines his head. 'No, we are in for some hot weather. At least we are better off today than tomorrow.'

'Why?' Jason wonders what Chanmi knows about the meeting the next day.

'Tomorrow will be a terrible day. Heat wave. Even here it will be unbearable.' He gulps down the rest of his juice and starts lacing up his brown and white shoes. They are pristine: even the eyelets on top and the spikes on the soles are shiny.

'Been playing much?' Jason asks.

Chanmi's head shudders. 'Last weekend, I did a round.'

'Big crowd?'

'Not a soul. I played very early. Here at ten-to-six.'

'In the dark, even?'

Chanmi stands up. 'Daybreak. Cool. Come, we'll go?'

He leads the way to the tee. He walks as if he is walking on eggshells, even though his shoes seem to weigh almost as much as he does. Jason follows, stepping down from the clubhouse with a little more confidence. The spikes clatter on the wood.

Their caddies are waiting by the tee. There are only a few other people about. Jason greets the caddies and Tito holds out his usual greenish driver and yellowing golf ball. Jason squeezes his hand into a grip-stained glove and then takes the club and ball. He fingers a red tee out of its holster.

Chanmi's clubs match his shoes; they could pass as brand new. His glove looks as if it is still warm from the calf's body.

'You go first,' Jason suggests.

Chanmi is not an elegant player. He wiggles and waggles a great deal and when he plays a stroke it is not very different from an extended wiggle. But he hits the ball gloriously. It flies straight as a bullet down the fairway and after its first bounce continues to shoot down almost to the water's edge.

'Excellent shot,' Jason murmurs. 'A good two hundred and twenty yards that. Auspicious or what?'

'Two-thirty in fact,' Chanmi corrects. 'I do this without fail on this hole.'

Jason's own ball hooks wickedly to the left. 'That too is a familiar stroke,' he announces with a little laugh. He picks up his smashed red tee and they set off down the fairway, the caddies following a few paces behind. Tito is chewing betel furiously; his lips beginning to turn Mars red. 'Sir,' he calls out, 'you think that the Britishers will really banish that Makarios to *our* country?'

At the water's edge Chanmi's caddie sucks his teeth in loud disapproval when Chanmi demands a five-iron. The caddie is incredulous, but hands the club over. The water is dark, as though it is a prehistoric, unfathomable lake, but in reality it is only knee-deep. The illusion of depth comes from the colour which, in turn, comes from the denseness of the brown water weeds. A boy combing the weeds with his toes brings out a ball for Jason. '*Adey*, your ball, sir,' Tito exclaims. Chanmi wiggles and waggles again over his small ball looking up at the green in short jerky movements. Then, for a brief second, he steadies himself before pulling his club back in a low, flat arc and hitting the ball and half a pound of clod up in the air. Both fly high; the clod dropping into the water like unwanted ballast and the ball barely making the ground on the far side. Chanmi's caddie spits into the water and replaces the divot with a camouflage of plucked grass while Chanmi strides ahead.

Jason plays a straight second shot which takes him to the edge of the green. He is pleased. 'Nice shot,' Chanmi taps him generously as they cross each other.

Jason's plan is to let Chanmi relax over five or six holes, and only then begin to talk business. *His* kind of business.

They play in their own solitary way for a number of holes. There is a lone player ahead of them; they keep right behind him. A foursome who had followed them off the first tee lag far behind by the time Jason and Chanmi reach the seventh.

After they both hole their balls and are walking away from the hopelessly bruised sunset towards the next tee, Jason asks Chanmi, 'So how are things with you?'

'I'm fine but my son has got mumps.'

'Oh-oh.'

'It's not a problem. I've had mumps. I'm immune. You have?'

Jason hesitates. 'I don't think so.'

'In that case, keep your distance. I could be a carrier. It's bad for your testicles, you know. Much more so than this Budego arrack.' Chanmi speaks like a doctor.

Jason touches his crotch, involuntarily. The sun is sinking fast. 'We'd better hurry,' he urges his companion.

They walk briskly. Jason's sweat is cooling, the sun is egging the whole sky, lapwings are shrieking '*did-u-do-it, did-u-do-it, did-u-do-it*' to disgruntled golfers, wayward partners and occasional murderers.

Jason couldn't help coming in with a better score than Chanmi although he had tried to downplay his game. To have played worse would have looked odd, but Chanmi looks satisfied with the result. He knows Jason is the better player and is happy to play with him in the hope that some of Jason's talent will rub off on him.

'How about a drink?' Jason pauses in front of the club-house.

'No, I think I'll go home.'

'Just one drink,' Jason insists, despite the danger of mumps. He needs to sow a few seeds, as it were, for the next day.

o

'Fantastic putting,' Jason compliments Chanmi when they sit down. 'It's like you know exactly how much force to put into motion.'

'Its mathematical, you know. The difficult part is the measuring.'

Chanmi would be down on all fours for every putt. He would place his ear on the ground and spend at least five seconds semi-prostrate.

'Are you listening for something when you put your ear to the ground?' Jason is genuinely interested. 'Or praying?'

Chanmi laughs, 'No, no. I go like that to look, you know. To get the ground-level view. I can tell the slope, you see, that way. Not the ear but the eye.'

'I thought you were measuring the sound of something to get the distance. The train, or water flowing, or something.'

Chanmi grins, pleased at his trick. 'No, I measure with my shoe. It is exactly ten inches long. And you see I have calibrated the edge of the sole so I can get an exact measurement.' Chanmi shows Jason his shoe, only slightly less sparkling than it had been before the game and their almost two-mile-long walk.

'I see.'

'Mathematics, you see. You need mathematics.'

Jason nods. He knows the need for mathematics, but he feels a greater need for something else at the moment: the power of persuasion. He looks at the brown bottle of beer between them; the glass is mottled with condensation.

'You want a chaser?' he offers. 'Scotch or something . . .'

'You mean your friend Budego's stuff?'

'If you really dare to drink it?'

Chanmi laughs. 'That's all nonsense in the newspaper. A fabrication. If there is any medical problem with liquor, it's with the vile hooch they produce around here, you know.'

'That's what I keep telling Eddy, but he won't listen.'

Chanmi grins again, in his small waspish way. 'Yes, dear Eddy.'

'You've seen the paper I did about Budego & Son?' Jason pauses.

'Hmm. Interesting.' Chanmi nods.

'You like the idea?'

'Jason, I don't think it is an emotional issue. Not a question of like or dislike. It is purely a question of gain or loss, long-term or short-term.'

'Or medium-term?'

'Yes, I think I mean what you mean by medium-term when I say long-term. I think for an emotional chap like you, long-term is more of metaphysical dimension. Am I right?'

Jason looks disappointed. It seems as though he is losing ground. 'All right. But do you agree with the assumptions? You see, I think the government will be facing some acute dilemmas in a few years' time: politics and economics are going to get thoroughly confused. Someone will wake up then to the fact that imported liquor is a real revenue earner, never mind its morally controversial nature, and should be taxed massively. Prices will become untenable. That's when a quality arrack will be highly desirable; unlike a twelve-year-old Malt it would have the allure of the attainable, and people will finally be proud of what we produce at home. And by then we could be producing the most delicious golden arrack ever – combining, like nobody else, the truly traditional with the efficiently modern. We don't have to have this cheap hooch like you said – the poison. They would never cut Scotch or cognac with formalin, would they? Why should we stand for it? After all, arrack is the first distilled alcohol in the history of the world, no?'

'Maybe.'

'It is. Or do you mean we should all poison ourselves? Forget quality and go for poison? Pretend this hooch is the best we can do?'

'No, I don't mean we should stick to . . .'

'Well then, shouldn't *we* develop the industry for all our benefit?'

'I suppose so.'

'So, will you support the proposal?'

'It is not for me to support, my friend. But I will do what is possible.'

DARKNESS

The art of what is possible . . . Jason underlined the phrase when he came to record it later that night.

○

That evening when Jason gets home, Pearl has already gone to the cinema.

Jinasena, the servant boy, tells him that Pearl has said she is going to be out for dinner as well. Jason goes to his room and bathes and changes.

Before leaving the house again, he sits down for a while on the veranda with a glass of water. Beyond his garden he can see the lights of his neighbours' houses burn. In front of him, Esra Vatunas's Bellevue glows between the gaps in the hedge of his garden. To the left, Tivoli Vatunas's upstairs lights cast tungsten oblongs across the lane. His lights were always on, whether Tivoli was in or not. The two houses seem to watch his own, waiting for the hours of darkness to pass. A momentary power blip makes the lights flicker and the shadows lengthen. The buildings seem to rock and shift closer.

At about eight-thirty Jason drives out along the coast road taking in the sea air. He goes a few miles south, towards the distillery in which he has invested so much of his vision of the future. In its vicinity there are a number of small lanes. He turns down one to where a small night market had begun recently: informal stalls that have sprung up to sell food and clothing, sometimes something illicit. Kerosene lamps light up each stall in red and yellow and the night seems even darker between each. The place is mostly full of men; there are bicycles and carts blocking most of the road. Jason eases his two-tone Hillman through the throng and reaches the centre of the market – a small crossroads. He turns right.

About a mile from the beach Jason comes to Srijan's temple of temporality. He stops the car by the gate. In the bungalow he can see more yellow light.

Later that night he writes in his blue book: *My whole life seems to have been heading for this moment, when some-how I will have to gather all my strength, all the energy of a lifetime, and force it into a single vision of what is going to happen next. I don't know how I am going to get through the next twenty-four hours. There is no one I can talk to any more.*

He takes a warm, feverish breath and opens the car door. *My head hurts.* He gets out and closes the door quietly. He walks up to Srijan's bungalow.

At the front steps he can see Srijan at his desk, reading. The sensuous face radiant in the rich yellow light. Jason coughs to announce his presence.

Srijan looks up and smiles.

'I need your help,' Jason peers forward, his head slowly bowing.

Srijan puts down his book and comes out onto the veranda. There are two benches and Srijan points to one. 'Sit down.'

They both sit in ritual silence for a minute or two. Jason stares at the wall in front of him, trying to make out the words he needs to say from Srijan's latest aphorism.

'What help?' Srijan inquires courteously.

'I feel tomorrow is going to be one of the most important days of my life.'

'It will be. It will be *the* most important day.'

'How do you know?'

Srijan smiles again. 'It will be.'

'Well then, maybe you know that tomorrow I will get my company to agree to take over the management of the Budego plant? If only my Chairman will give me what I need.'

'And what would that be?'

'Support. He can't see what is going on yet.'

'And you can?'

'I have my suspicions. They can't stop me. I will get the distillery working properly again in time for the new season. Your people around here will have work.'

Srijan's lashless lids drop over his eyes. 'You call it work?'

Jason leans forward with his elbows on his knees. He

clasps his hands together trying to lock his fingers into each other. 'What else?'

'They work on this poison, and for what?'

'It will not be poison. It will be a true water of life.'

'*L'eau de vie*?'

'Yes. I want to do what is best. My problem is how to *know* what is really for the best.'

'Do what you were going to do before you stopped here,' Srijan advises quietly.

'I was going to the beach.'

'And?'

'I was going to walk on the sand.'

'And?'

'Listen to the ocean.'

'So do it.'

○

Jason parks his car on a grass verge by the railway tracks. There is a brittle wooden gate marking the end of the road and the beginning of the railway line with its thick, heavy blackened sleepers and heaps of broken stones. Beyond these are dark straggly coconut trees: several fused by bolts of lightning into decapitated stumps, and the others gangly with the confusion of sea winds that whip around the headland. Between the spiralling ghostly trunks, thick brush and matted grass grow in darkness until they give way to the sea creepers reaching out to the surf like the long shadows of extinct trees.

The sea itself is not discernible: there is sky and only sky, diving almost into blackness with dark clouds that seem to seethe into the darker clouds of the ocean.

The gate swings open on a piece of twisted wire. Jason goes through and steps on to the rusted iron rails. He stands on tiptoe, as if testing it for give; a mirror-band of steel on ancient shifting sand.

He likes to come to this spot from time to time because of its utter darkness. If the moon is veiled, then the tracks only gleam under his feet. To his right and to his left they vanish into black holes. He is faced with the silhouettes of dead trees, shadows without light, and the roar of an invisible sea. It is a place where vision could fail but the senses come alive: the smell of the sea, the roar of water and wind. The fronds of dead and dying trees. But after a little while the eye begins to learn to see again. To discern shapes out of the darkness, tell the sea from the sky and entrap the imagination. *The imagination is our most molested flower*, he wrote, *so easily crippled in a heartless paradise*.

On this night, when Jason reaches the beach he notices that a few hundred yards further down there is the glow of a campfire. He can see figures moving in front of it and their voices, like Eddy Kaduwira's, carry the sound of irresponsible laughter. There are several beach huts – mat-and-tat rattan rooms – along the curve of the bay. He turns away; he finds their existence increasingly intrusive, but when he looks in the other direction he can see chips of light in the sea. A ship heading towards an invisible port. People on the move, the roll of the sea. He remembers the anniversary but it is too late.

IX

SEVEN-THIRTY

Up in my guest room Prins had fallen asleep.

Pearl never seemed to sleep. Perhaps it was because she never travelled; at least, at the time that I got to know her. She had travelled in a once-and-for-all migration (with the one reconnaissance of the route in 1938), but for the rest of her life she seemed inert. She didn't move much; and so, perhaps, she didn't sleep much. Everything around her moved: pictures on her TV screen, the earth, the moon, but Pearl herself was quite sedentary. And in the winter she said she liked to hibernate. This meant she would sit with a shawl around her shoulders and watch whatever was on TV, with only an occasional look out of the front window to check the flow of bicycles, cars and people going along Almeida Avenue. 'Sand in Batter*sea*,' she chuckled when London's power failed and everything ground to a halt in the opening scene of the 1936 thriller, *Sabotage*.

The winter before Prins left her, Pearl had bought herself a bag-suit to sit in.

'What the hell is that?' Prins practically turned his face inside out when he walked in and saw her.

'A body warmer,' Pearl snuggled in.

'Where'd you find such a daft thing?'

'I got it from that catalogue, you know? That catalogue with all those funny gadgets you go on about.' She looked at me for corroboration.

'You can't just sit like that. Like a sack of potatoes.'

Pearl stood up in her glorified sleeping bag and shuffled over to the window. 'It keeps me warm. When you are older you will realize how necessary it is to keep warm. *Warm*.' Her eyes were shining.

But snow excited her too.

'This is what I love,' she would say to me when the first snow of the winter fell in London, invariably in her garden before anywhere else. She would celebrate by opening a bottle of brandy, whatever time it started, and cutting into her Christmas cake. It didn't matter whether it happened before Christmas or after, morning, noon or night; the event was always celebrated the same way.

Her hair was white and her skin a waxy yellow. When she lit her candles on Christmas Eve, she became like one herself. Lit up. She would light a candle for each person in the house. If anybody dropped in she would always light another candle and place it on the table. Her Christmas cake was always black and wet, as if it was made in the dark in a barrel of brandy. People would reel after a bite, and become instantly talkative, unless it happened to be Ravi.

'Wonderful cake,' they would say, brightening up.

Pearl would smile knowingly. 'My secret recipe.' She made it on the cusp of autumn and winter. Early, in case the snow came early.

Making the cake was a big affair. For two days it would dominate the kitchen. A huge mixing bowl would sit in the middle of the kitchen table like a bottomless well. Tons of ingredients would be chucked in: bags of raisins, heaps of currants, mixed fruit, cherries. The year I lived in her house I was given the task of shopping for the cake. I came back laden with four carrier bags, my fingers white with the weight of the shopping. Everything went into the bowl. I could not understand how one bowl could contain it all.

After two days of mixing and stirring and wheeling the ingredients, she would bake the cake and then it would disappear for weeks leaving only the tantalizing scent of almond essence and rose water. She would hide it until Christmas or snow, whichever came first, but every room in the flat would reek of it.

That last Christmas Eve she had only one candle lit when I dropped by. A perfect flame pointing to heaven. 'Naomi said she'll come later with Dylan,' Pearl mumbled as though she had to explain the weakness of the light. 'You want some cake? I thought I'd cut it tonight anyway, while you are here.'

She produced a big square biscuit tin and opened it. 'I love these tins,' she said, revealing a cake covered with a snowfall of sugar.

'You made this on your own?' I asked.

She laughed, wheezing. 'Why, who else is here to make it?' She lifted it out. 'Dylan brought me the raisins and all. And a big bottle of cognac. He comes every few days, you know.' She lit a second candle, cupping her hand to the flame, and placed it next to the first. 'Such a *nice* boy.' She cut a slice. There was no snow yet.

There were two more candles unlit, waiting on the table.

o

While Prins dozed, I sat alone and remembered collecting Mira in a freak blizzard to drive over to Almeida Avenue for a full-house winter rice and curry.

Mira was on a bed with black sheets. Her hair was wet. Her face was scrubbed and raw. Her head, weighed down on one side by three heavy silver earrings and no compensating ballast on the other, sank into her elongated neck. She hunched her shoulders, 'Fuck.'

I put down my mug of hot tea on top of a frosted TV.

'Look at these,' she held a pair of neon legwarmers. 'The fucking elastic's completely gone. Why do they make crap like this?' Mira looked at me, defying me.

On her clapped-out radio Elton John and Kiki Dee sang 'Don't Go Breakin' My Heart'; Mira kicked the radio and the batteries burst out of its belly. 'Stupid bastard.'

'Who?' I asked, knowing full well who it was.

'Prins. Who else?' Mira was cross about Prins's new plan to up and leave, as if by invoking his dream of returning to his ancestral island he was debasing her own dream of flight and escape. 'Don't you think he is stupid?' Her voice scraped the air.

'Why does he want to go there? Why suddenly? And like forever? He talks as if he has to go forever, or never at all. Isn't that stupid?'

'It's to do with the chromosomes of the mind,' I quoted Prins.

'Fucking stupid attitude,' Mira muttered, choosing her words carefully. She pulled on a big, green, man's jumper. 'What I need is a break,' Mira pouted. 'A real break, like moneybags, not a frigging snowstorm.'

On the other side of the road scaffolding was thickening with the snow: tubular bells growing a geometric cancer.

'I can't think straight,' she said. 'I can't stay still. Everything is always jumping. Do you feel that, sometimes? Everything is like a pinprick.' She looked around her, furtively, as if she might have to fly. 'Or is it just me?'

'I don't know,' I said. In those days, I was not so jumpy.

'It's just that if I stop for a sec, I feel I'm going to get pushed over. All these sounds hammering away, people pushing in at the edges. Do you know what I mean? It's like so *crowded* everywhere.'

O

'I got a new job!' Prins exclaimed the moment we arrived. Mira stamped feverishly about, dusting snow from her boots. Harry Belafonte was singing 'Island in the Sun' out of an antique record-player in Pearl's yellow sitting room. I could not believe he had moved so fast in his plans to abandon us and go.

'There?' I asked.

'No, not there. Here.'

Pearl shuffled across to the kitchen. 'That's the way with him, always a riddle.'

'You are not going then?' Mira leaned forward as if stretching out to nibble something.

'I didn't say I wasn't going. But until I go, I've got a job.' He stepped into the kitchen and picked up two glasses from the trolley. 'Management consultant.'

'What do you know about management?' Mira looked disgusted.

Prins laughed. 'It's so easy. You just listen and repeat. Tape-recorder job.'

Ravi, who was quietly opening the door into his room, pricked up his ears.

Prins explained how he had been speaking to a friend of his in the consultancy business who had mentioned a problem they had over a new contract; the consultant they had had lined up had run away to Sydney with an Australian ballet-boy. They needed someone with experience of the clothing retail business. Prins said he was their man. He had been interviewed by three men bursting out of their blue suits and Van Heusen striped shirts: a grey stripe, a blue stripe and, in the centre, a red stripe. Prins gave them a lecture on cost-effective clothing purchase and they appointed him. The man in the red stripe had cracked his knuckles every time Prins said *stripe*. He had bifocals through which he squinted to check that all his fingers still remained in place after each gigantic crunch.

'I had them in a piggy-bind,' Prins laughed. 'His bloody knuckles went Persil-white when I said how much dough I wanted. But they had no choice by then.'

'How did you know how much to ask for, *la*?' Tripti smiled sweetly at Prins, always eager for useful titbits.

Prins laughed again. 'These guys – you know, when you start talking it just turns so real for them. Whatever you say, they believe. The corporate world is *schlock*-full of unsatisfied believers; they go for anything new. New words that mean old things. They love words that massage their egos.' He shook his head. 'You guys don't understand what is going on in this place. Everything is turning upside down. Everyone wants low-cost, OK? Anything public has to be shoe-string stuff: roads, schools, libraries. In Government they'll talk of quality, but they mean cheap-cheap. But in *this* business everything hangs on the big price. You pay a lot – then you value it. For a thousand quid, even shit smells wonderful. Nice trick, huh?'

Mira was unusually quiet. She seemed to be communing with her beer. She would sometimes go into this deep silence, staring straight ahead of her as if she was steeling herself for something. She would stay still, a phase noticeable in her unlike in most people because she was usually so jumpy. After a couple of minutes of this silence though, she would suddenly blurt out whatever was on her mind. 'Corporate berk!'

'Mira!' Tripti whined. 'Don't be like that, *la*.'

Mira tossed her head back and ran her fingers through her short, flat hair. 'It's true. He's gonna be a berk.' She stood up and shook herself, then marched into the kitchen to Pearl.

Prins laughed and rubbed the imaginary notes between his fingers. 'Only for a few months. Then I'll be a *rich* berk.'

○

As it turned out Prins stayed corporate for almost a year. He got out only by running away. But it was not long before he shot back into it in Sri Lanka: selling the paradise experience between death camps and suicide bombers to tourists who didn't care.

But at that time we all believed that nothing ever lasted beyond a few months. And it didn't matter. It was a source of comfort that life would change. That nothing would remain the same. We believed things were going to get better, not worse. Prins believed this passionately. He would talk about the future as though it was a place to get to; and that once you reached it, everything would be set out as you would have wanted. Life was like a motorway on a perfectly articulated road map. It was all there to see. The only problem was getting the right car to take you all the way to the ultimate smorgasbord, and fast enough.

It was a very different picture of the world from that of

his mother, Pearl. For her there was no map. All the places belonged either to the present or the past. The future was a fantasy. In her yellow room in Almeida Avenue she would rather watch a horror movie, any time of the day or night, than think about the future.

○

After Pearl's huge, buttery lunch, Mira immediately wanted to slide down to the nearest pub.

'Yes, you people go,' Pearl urged. 'Go. They say the new wine bar on the corner by the traffic lights is very fine.'

'How d'you know?' Prins snapped at his mother, unable to restrain his filial irritation.

Pearl shrugged her round shoulders, ignoring his rudeness. Her whole body seemed to ripple with the waters of the deep. 'Never mind how. I know. I have eyes, you know, and ears.'

'Serendipity is it, aunty?' Tripti piped in. 'I know they do great cocktails – pineapple *Superman*.'

'Great,' Mira croaked. 'I'm always in the market for a superman, any kind of man . . .' She looked at Tripti and suppressed a laugh. 'But where's our Professor La Trappe? Come on babes.'

Ravi had already slunk into his room and locked the door. Wild horses couldn't drag him out.

'Never mind him,' Prins pressed close to Mira and lifted her by the waist. 'This session's strictly for Mira's superman.'

'Let me down,' Mira squealed. 'Let's go, let's go. Come on *Cheep*.'

That was my cue, but I shrank back. It was all too much for me. I said I would stay back to do the dishes. I knew that Pearl had another Hitchcock movie in mind. I preferred to watch it with her; melt back into that cosy world of temporary terror and listen to the stories of other places and other times that it would release from Pearl. 'You guys go,' I mumbled, 'I've had enough snow for now.'

'You just want aunty's cream sherry, no?' Mira taunted.

'Go, go,' Pearl shooed them out. 'Put the TV, *putha*,' she said as soon as they had gone. 'It's *Suspicion*. Cary Grant and Joan Fontaine.'

o

Even in Shangri-La, back in 1991, Prins was quite taken with the Vatunases as a family. I think he envied the richness of their story more than their wealth. He discovered so much about their lives, through Lola, that it made up for the paucity of the facts about his own family's past. I remember him talking about Tivoli and his sons, especially Dino, with a surprising sense of awe. We were at the empty emerald poolside of his Shangri-La. Below us the hill dropped to a river, more of sand than water, lined by enormous trees as sombre as tombstones.

'Fifteen years after grandfather Esra died, while you and I were swinging our pricks about in London, Dino turned himself into a mega-boss. By then Tivoli, his father, had learned to become rather more fond of the product than the production process of the new Vatunas business empire: he would polish off a bottle of Vambrosia every two days with his eyes closed.'

In his younger days Tivoli Vatunas, like most of his social contemporaries, scorned the local *pol*-arrack. He would refuse to touch it. 'He was known among my father's circle of friends as the man who said that he preferred a pot of turpentine to an unsavoury Ambrose tot,' Prins reported. But he was a light drinker then.

Tivoli started to get seriously into drinking in 1967, after his mother, Delia, died. He moved into Bellevue – where she had lived alone for five years after Esra died – and discovered that it suited him perfectly. Even the Vambrosia. He found a bottle of the first Vatunas-Budego blend in his father's – now his – study. He had stared at it for longer than he had ever stared at his father's grave, or even his mother's. Eventually he grabbed it and twisted open the top. 'For the first time in my life the aroma of coconut in it smelled somehow mine, rather than my father's,' Prins quoted from a Dino anecdote about Tivoli. 'He poured two inches of the famous amber liquid and found it slipped down his throat more easily and more pleasantly than he had ever imagined.' Two weeks later he had finished the bottle.

For several months, almost a year, he drank his liquor at the rate of about a bottle every two weeks – a bottle drunk on his own, not counting the social drinking that he indulged in as the head of a large corporation. But after the first year he picked up speed. The bottles began to empty faster and faster. His eyes became more and more water-logged.

In his last years Tivoli would mutter constantly that he had at least produced the descendants that were demanded of him, as though the siring of them had taken too many beats out of his heart. By the time Dino took over Tivoli was slightly inebriated most of his waking hours. 'Sozzled stupid,' as Prins would put it. 'Tivoli felt trapped between his father and his son. His only solace was in the bottle, where he could ignore Dino crowding him as Esra had done. But Dino was the only one who really cared about Esra's empire.'

By then Dino's older brother, Kia, had developed a serious aversion to most of his father's enterprises. Kia had moved to a house on the other side of the compound, as far as possible from the house he had been born in, while remaining within the bounds of his inheritance. Buppy, the youngest son, had turned into a wastrel addicted to illegal gambling and Mariakadé prostitutes. Tivoli had never quite recognized him. And Lola had gone abroad to Manchester to study art. Education was all Tivoli ever intended to provide for her, and he must have felt magnanimous for giving her the opportunity he was never offered as an artist; in any case, he saw her as his wife's proper responsibility, because being female he did not expect her to remain a Vatunas once she grew up.

'Kia, Lola's favourite, is the weirdest of them all. He hates me. He was born-again last year,' Prins's face hardened in the light reflected off the surface of the swimming pool. 'You see, he killed a man in a hunting accident back in 1971. Money, property and timing protected Kia, much as they destroyed the poor sod who had come into his line of fire.' The whole affair was subsumed and conveniently forgotten by the authorities in the carnage of the following weeks, when the countryside was convulsed in killing of a more ferocious nature as the army and police frantically suppressed their first post-colonial insurrection. 'Kia was left with only himself to deal with. When he finally converted not only did it change his life, but it unhinged the Vatunases. The two older brothers were well and truly bifurcated.' Kia built a ten-foot wall around his house; the west was cut off from the east. He did what he thought was necessary in a world of iniquity, but Prins believed Kia was deranged.

Dino, on the other hand, was always a smooth operator. He liked control but showed no desire to be the centre of mass attention. Unlike his father, and his father's father before him, Dino worked through a dedicated team of lieutenants. These were specially selected technocrats whose entire self-esteem was based on Dino's judgement. He was a master at freeing himself of the burdens of responsibility while retaining ultimate control and command. The Vatunas enterprise flourished under him. He freed the company from the family, sold shares in it and widened the composition of the Board (including even some individuals from Sanderson Bros.). But everyone knew that if Dino wanted something to happen, it would happen. Other people would always fall in line.

The day before we were due to leave Shangri-La and go down to Colombo to spend a few days at another of Prins's hotels, Dino's secretary called him. 'Out of the blue, *men*,' Prins hissed. 'An invitation to visit Dino at his office. That weird Vatunas building.' I shook the pool water out of my ear and, on Prins's advice, rubbed sunscreen on my shoulders. 'Tuesday afternoon, will you come? Give some moral support? I don't know what he wants. Lola's not here.'

'Don't go if you don't want to,' I advised.

'But Dino is *the* man now. Has a finger in every bloody arsehole in this country. You can't do anything without him. I must go.' He seemed quite exhilarated by the prospect.

'Dino has his head screwed on right. Clever fellow,' Prins said with a slight twitch of his neck. 'This guy can smell money a hundred miles away. You should see even the way he walks.' Prins shifts his head from side to side as though it was disjointed. 'Those two older brothers – Kia and Dino – were always fighting as kids. Kia was a big fellow, Dino was all pluck. He could throw him. Physically push the guy out of the way.'

But Dino was the first of the modern Vatunases to turn to fat. His face is sharp and sure and his eyes dart above a disarming smile, but from the neck down Dino spreads out. Despite his shape, he can still move swiftly when he wants to. He is Colombo's most surreal power-boy. Perhaps it was he, and not Kia, who had discovered the true route to salvation: metamorphosis.

As a child, even though he was not the first grandson, Dino was always his grandfather Esra's favourite. When Dino was just ten years old Esra took him to the Vatunas central office. He took him by the hand, much to the surprise and delight of Delia. 'I want to show the boy a thing or two,' he had said to her. Tivoli had not made his peace with Esra at the time and Dino seemed to leapfrog into his place. At the Vatunas headquarters Esra told Dino that in every room of the building, and there were thirty-three of them, there was at least one person working for his future. 'Do you know what I mean?'

Dino had said, 'No, *Siya*. What do you mean working for *my* future?'

The old man was not used to explaining himself; his life was all about creating mysteries, but he had wanted to give somebody a clue. Dino was the one he had selected; he was the one who gave the old man most hope. He wanted to plant something in the child's mind that would make sense years later. An emotional talisman that would bring Esra and his dream back to life one day, in Dino's transition from child to man.

'Never mind,' he had said. 'All you need to remember is that there are a lot of people for whom your name – our name – is a livelihood. And remember, they are here because of me, just like you.'

The doorman, the peons, the secretaries and the office workers passing by them bowed to the old man and smiled at the child; Dino did not smile back. He watched them. He had no idea what they were doing but he knew from what his grandfather had said that they were doing it all because of some hold the Vatunases had over their lives – even their smiles signalled the precariousness of their livelihoods.

Esra took him to the top floor, his grand office. He pushed him in through the solid wood mandala doors. 'Look out of the window,' he had said to Dino. 'Can you see? This is the town in which you will be king.'

There was a reverential knock on the door. Esra had barked out, 'Yes.'

A man in a white shirt and blue tie came in. 'Excuse me, sir. There is one thing, sir.'

'What?'

'Srijan called up, sir.'

'What did he say?'

'He said that the fellows are now OK, sir. Everyone is happy.'

'Good.' Esra turned away from the man and went to the window and stood next to his grandson. 'Everyone is happy,' he had sung softly to the boy. 'Everyone is happy.' Dino repeated it to Lola: 'Everyone is happy now.'

Outside they could see a spread of older office blocks with large shade-trees in-between. Esra's own building was on new development land. As always, he wanted to be the path-breaker. He had bought the land and built a new building taller than anything else in the surrounding area, in the sure knowledge that others would follow in his hammer-headed wake and increase the value of his property. From his office you could see a canal, a lake, and in the distance even a thin strip of sea and a few coconut trees. 'Water,' he had hissed. Water was what was important.

'Are you also happy, *Siya*?' Dino had pulled at his grandfather's sleeve.

The old man sucked in his lips and tested his teeth against them. He stared straight ahead at the horizon for a moment before answering. Then he put his hand on his grandson's shoulder, cupping the small bone in a wiry tangle of tendons and ageing cartilage. 'Yes, I am getting happy too. But it doesn't come easy, boy. You remember that. It doesn't come easy.'

o

On the day we were to meet Dino, Prins picked me up from Mount Lavinia and we drove over to the tightly guarded monolithic Vatunas building. He jabbed me in the ribs, 'Now, whatever you do, don't ask him about his brothers.'

From the reception desk a polished young woman with thickly braided hair took us down to what seemed a vast air-conditioned underground extension. She showed us to a pair of New Wave chairs at one end and disappeared into a dark recess in the middle of the strategically spot-lit floor.

'Swish bunker, no?' Prins tested the tension of his chair. We lingered in uneasy silence until a few minutes later when Dino opened what I had thought was an ebony-panelled wall to reveal his presidential suite. 'So, how?' he greeted Prins in a low growl. We stepped in.

Prins introduced me. Dino smiled coldly. 'Good. Sit down. Coffee? Or a Special?'

'Oh, not a Special. I'll have a coffee. I've just been at the opening of a brand new karaoke bar – big bucks.' Prins swaggered. His voice was louder than normal, as if he was trying to hide something.

Dino watched Prins but said nothing. He slipped his thumbs into his waistband and stretched it another half inch in preparation for further expansion.

'Japanese investment,' I piped up, and they both turned towards me. Two pairs of eyes staring straight into me. There was an uncanny resemblance between them; something to do with the intensity of each eye perhaps, or the configurations behind them. 'Yen,' I said as if by way of explanation. 'Not bucks, yen.'

Prins drank his coffee as if it was an act of survival. Dino shifted his eyes in my direction and then turned his head almost as an afterthought. 'You play golf?' he asked me softly.

I rocked my hand. 'Not very well.'

'Prins, you a good player, no?'

Prins was noncommittal. 'I play a little.'

'I need a good golfer. A negotiator. Lola told me you play.'

'You don't play? I saw your father's name at the club.'

Dino raised an eyebrow. 'Such a time-waster. I don't see the point of putting a ball in a hole. Walking half a mile to do it.'

Prins laughed nervously and played with his hands, clasping one with the other. He couldn't crack knuckles yet.

'But you see, your friend is right,' Dino nodded generously in my direction. 'After thirty years of Japan-talk, we finally have the Japanese coming here. A genuine golfer on our side could be valuable.' Dino showed his teeth in a perfunctory smile. 'Very *nice*.'

'You want to sell Vambrosia in Japan?'

'Why not? It's a matter of marketing the taste; designing a bottle that fits the palm of every hand.'

'You want me to join Vatunas?'

'Why not?'

'What would your brother, Kia, think? And Buppy?' Prins brought them in, after warning me not to. But Dino didn't flinch. He brought in his sister instead. 'Lola would be pleased. And we are all interested in the same thing.'

I wondered what Pearl would have made of it, sitting in her yellow room in London, watching an electric bar glow and a spider descend towards it, a slice of date and walnut cake in her arthritic fingers: her son bridging the gulf between the Ducals and this progressive generation of the scheming Vatunases.

When we eventually stumbled out of the Vatunas vault into the sunshine outside, Prins was full of admiration. 'That guy Dino really has style.' He nodded to himself. 'The golf is a good sign.'

I wasn't so sure. 'What was that business about you all being interested in the same thing? Hotels?'

'Lola, his sister,' Prins sighed in exasperation. 'How can I carry on a feud forever. Esra's generation is gone, gone, gone. Look at it, will you? I love that girl, no? And Dino is the guy who can help me get everything I want for her, as well as for me.'

A few days later Prins was on the golf course playing above his handicap to please the future tipplers and swillers of the export-quality, bottled in blue china, Vambrosia de luxe special.

o

'Lola and I met here at this same table over *business*, you know,' Prins confided. We were at the Harbour Room, on the top floor of the Grand Oriental, looking out over the barricaded high-security Customs Office of the deserted port. Beyond the whitewashed building the sea puckered; its blue skin wrinkled by the lives of all those who worried at its fathomless face – like us from a distance in a tall building, or from a ship's rail, or from the water's edge, wanting to retreat before it is too late.

Prins finished his Vam-an'-Lime and smacked his lips. He said he had wanted to develop a modern cultural identity alongside the traditional tourist industry on the island. 'I am fed up to the back molars with bloody Tuesday night fire-eating, and hopscotch on burning coals. And every bleeding Sunday night the same old conch-fart and *hewisi-*stomp. These tourists think all we have here is handicraft and folk artists. All they get is *jaggerified* cultural twaddle. Twenty-year-old pop songs played by decrepit combos in dance rooms more boring than a piss-pot museum and handicraft, handicraft, handicraft.' Prins banged his fist into his hand. 'I want them to feel something contemporary, you know. Modern art. Street theatre. TV shows, cartoons. Anything with a pulse. We are at the crossroads of the whole world and what do we offer that's new? Goose-steps and bloody goon squads. Is that all we are now?'

He had started with the idea of a series of contemporary art exhibitions, linked to a prize. 'I told these guys, let's get some energy into this dump. Why shouldn't people come here from Singapore or Tokyo and buy art? Why do we think only the Europeans – the Germans and the Swiss – will come, just for a beach? Sex, sun and sand, there's no damn future in it.' He could see it even then: sex would turn unsafe, the sun would become cancerous, and the sand slowly slip into the sea leaving behind only a squalid line of tarted-up pleasure domes.

He got a few business cronies to see the potential for profiteering from art. They bought in: prize money, hotel venues, businessmen's banquets.

Lola Vatunas happened to be the artist he met first. It was a meeting arranged by one of his business partners.

'We just knew immediately. I hadn't seen her since that time in Birkenhead, but we knew.' Prins grinned, 'It sounds corny, I know, but at least it was not at first sight.'

o

The first time I met Lola was with Prins at Tripti's parents' home in the summer of 1978. We had driven there, with Mira sprawled in the back seat, to meet one of the few remaining relatives of Pearl and Prins that any of us knew about – Baresh, the sailor boy. He had become a mate on a foreign ship and was docking in at Liverpool on his first trip to Europe. Prins had suggested to his mother that they drive up to see him, but Pearl would not travel. 'How can I go so far?' She had wrinkled up her nose as if she had never stepped out of the house since coming to London on her own. 'He can come here, if he wants. He is the great voyager, not me.'

Baresh was a huge, round man with a thick mass of a beard. 'A bison,' Prins suggested later. 'Not a bosun but a bison.' He did have that look about him: an enormous head on a ball of a body, the whole thing about to roll over anything that stood in its way. Snorting and heaving his shoulders, lowering his head with his large eyes swivelling like magnetic pinheads. How he ducked and weaved that bulk of his among the rabbit runs and ducting, the bulwark of his decrepit cargo boat was impossible to imagine. He filled the whole hatch when he peered out of his cabin to see us. 'Prins,' he bellowed. 'You must be Prins, Pearl's Prins. Yes?'

Prins grinned and nodded.

'Come in, come in,' Baresh urged. 'My God, *men*, I have not seen you since you were a little pip-squeak hanging onto your sister's frock.'

He unplugged himself from the doorway and we bobbed in. The cabin was surprisingly spacious. Partly the effect of Baresh appearing to shrink as he wedged himself into a peculiar corner seat. It was an armchair that seemed specially designed to fit into a right-angle. 'Sit, sit,' he called out as he sank into place, adjusting himself into a triangle with a vastly distended hypotenuse.

'I was speaking to your mother,' Baresh's voice boomed in his chrome-studded cabin. 'She said you were driving up.'

'Yes, we have a friend up here. We thought we'd hit both of you in one shot.' Prins grinned. 'We spun up last night.'

Baresh flicked a fridge door open with the little finger of his left hand. He lobbed can after can at Prins and me. 'Beer,' he said as if he was naming the birds and the bees. 'Want a coke?' he asked Mira. I saw her tense up. She grabbed a beer. She was the first to hiss a can open, half tipping it towards him.

'So, you have friends in this Liverpool?'

'Birkenhead.' Mira licked the froth off her fingers.

'What?'

'Birkenhead. On the other side of the Mersey.'

Mira said there were docks there too. Baresh nodded slowly, his eyes narrowing further as though he was trying to follow a word game, or the conventions of a new language. Above him I could see a shelf with a yellow, laughing Buddha. Small, squat, big-bellied and round-headed. He stood with his feet firmly apart and his short arms aloft as if he was holding up the ceiling. His head was slightly inclined, a bit like the earth tilting for spring, a huge grin opening the fat face – but unusually, a face that seemed friendly and pleasant, rather than leering from the edge of enlightenment. I felt he was attempting the impossible, like all of us: holding up the sky while standing on water. Next to it lay the *Tibetan Book of the Dead* and a mail-order catalogue.

'You know, I have not seen your mother for more than twenty years, since your *Thaththi's* funeral,' Baresh burped. 'What a scene that was. She really was the talk of the town then. Gave those Colombo *mudalalis* and the police and the newspapers absolute hell – she was wonderful. She was the one who got your father to help me get on a ship, before the poor chap got shot. "Get out of this hole and see the world," she told me, when all I wanted was to see your sis. She was seventeen and *out* of this world.' He closed an eye, salaciously. 'Your mother and my father were second cousins, I think. So that makes us what?'

Prins looked at me, I looked at Mira. We had no idea. Mira, with her phobia of families, least of all.

'What the hell, anyway. I suppose we are all related one way or the other.' Baresh swallowed the rest of his beer and crushed the can in his fist. 'Another beer? Or you fellows want to tour the ship?'

Outside, I heard Prins invite him to Tripti's mother's house where we were staying. She had suggested a get-together in the evening with Lola there as well.

Lola had come to Birkenhead for the weekend to get away from her college in Manchester. She had known Tripti, or her mother, through some esoteric Lankan–Singaporean connection. She said she was fed up with drawing pregnant women and limp dicks: life classes were on the wane. Her escape route was the commuter line from Oxford Road to Lime Street, a snatch of 'Penny Lane' in the air and then she'd nip down under Lewis's infamous bronze scrotum and catch a train below the Mersey heading for New Brighton, Wallasey or Rock Ferry. 'Despite the Cavern and all that,' she said, smoking a neat, pink Sobranie in Tripti's mother's garden, 'on this side I feel I am at the real edge. I can see the sea. A way out.' Lola gave the impression of always looking to escape. She had long lanky hair that streamed across her face as though she was constantly in the slipstream of another planet.

The garden we sat in that afternoon was small but full of sunlight. It was on the edge of an open heath of wild heather and pewter rocks, fringed with birch woods and pines. The garden had a curve to it that seemed to give it more sky than we were used to in London, and perhaps more than Lola was used to in Manchester. There were foxgloves in the garden and a vegetable patch that seemed to be a monstrous caricature of a storybook garden: unearthed onions that had grown out of proportion, lettuce shot through to the aurora borealis, corn cobs bursting like

Aztec rockets. Lola sat on a child's red swing, smoking through a net of fine hair, watching Prins and me.

She talked to me more than Prins in that garden, but I could barely hear her; she spoke in a teasing whisper most of the time. Her lips would move but produce more smoke than sound. I listened, bending forward, resting my head on my hand and surreptitiously cupping an ear, not wanting to interrupt the almost inaudible plume of murmuring in case it stopped in shock. She burbled about Post-Impressionists and neo-classical tarts; she seemed annoyed by the history of art and had a thing about blue. 'Blue,' she puffed as if it was the last word on the subject, unaware, as I was, of how fast that colour would seem to wash through all our lives: Ravi's, Jason's, Pearl's and even mine. I asked her where she came from before Manchester. 'Is your family here?' I had no idea who she was at the time. 'Cannibals,' she simpered. 'I've run away from cannibals.' She took another drag and then stretched out her neck to look over me around the garden. Her small breasts rose in a rush of silk. She said nothing more after that.

At the other end of the garden Mira, softened by the sun, had stripped down to her T-shirt. She lay on the grass and stared at a dwarf apple tree. I saw her pick up a windfall. I was suddenly aware that we were each on our own there, drawn to one another, looking for something we could not talk about, and yet content to wait. Like the magnolia, the apple tree, the bed of poppies in that warm garden, each separate, and yet together somehow making something improbably unique. Prins, Mira, Lola, Tripti and I all still for once: anything seemed possible and nothing too much to expect.

After a while we drifted into the makeshift conservatory where tea had been poured. Lola stroked my hand lightly and disappeared inside the house while Mira and I had a cup of Mrs Krishnaraj's highly refined tea.

'Just like up-country, no?' Mira lapsed into the accent of her past, losing her effs momentarily and spinning helplessly homeward. The fresh air, the smell of pine, the sense of a cool earth temporarily warmed, made the place seem high up.

Lola came back and giggled when I mentioned how high up we seemed, but she didn't actually say anything. She pinched her lips with her fingers and perched on a chair. She had her blouse neatly buttoned right down to her slender wrists. Her eyes looked dreamy, a slight flicker that suggested she was watching something that none of the rest of us could see.

'Christ! It's hot in here,' Mira drained her tea and headed for the door. Lola hardly noticed. But she was startled when the refrigerator in the corner whinnied. Tripti opened it and put away the blue and white jug of milk. 'Let's go for a walk,' she said brightly. 'The woods are wonderful. Mira, you'll love it.'

I wanted to walk with Mira but she had already taken Prins's arm. Lola seized my hand. We went out of the front gates down the main road for a few yards before entering the birch woods. There was a small trail lined with gorse bushes leading uphill. I held Lola's elbow, vainly trying to catch her low murmuring.

'You get a wonderful view of the city from the top,' Tripti called out as if she could detect some reluctance on the part of Prins and Mira.

I asked Lola whether she had been up the hill before. 'Always.' She looked at me with such freshness that I was taken aback.

'What do you mean?'

'I always come here, when I come here . . .' She cupped her hands around her mouth and lit another cigarette. This time a baby-blue one.

'How many colours do they come in?'

She pressed closer to me and opened her flat cigarette case of rainbow Sobranies. 'Sometimes I light up one of my pastel sticks by mistake,' she smirked as if slightly drunk. Her breath was ultra-sweet.

We climbed some small rocks and reached a plateau of heather and stone. On the left there was a large pond with ducks. Prins had his arms around both Tripti and Mira. I sat down on the branch of a tree away from the others, and Lola moved on ahead. She picked at some heather but then strayed towards the edge of the cliff. I ran over, but when I got to her she blithely pointed at the cityscape before us: Liverpool with a slightly burnt coating. A flat sprawl of blackened buildings with its two cathedrals pitted against the sky. 'Look,' she tittered. 'Those are moving.'

A small block of windows reflected light and seemed to slide.

'It's a ship.' I said. Could it be Baresh's?

She tittered some more and held onto me again like a small girl from another world. 'I know that Prins,' she blushed. '*Prins.*' But I couldn't be sure of her words, or what she meant at the time.

o

By the time Baresh arrived we had opened the beer. Everyone drank beer except Lola; she wanted green tea. She spent most of that evening with a coloured stick in her hand, alternating Sobranies with Crayolas. She did a small landscape of the hill we had climbed in the afternoon: a few strips of colour on a piece of card about the size of a cigarette packet. It was remarkable, but most of her conversation remained inaudible, at least to me, although

Prins must have caught something that stayed with him for all these years.

I preferred to get Baresh to talk more about Pearl after what he had said on the ship about her antics in Colombo, but he only wanted to describe his journey around the world. Mrs Krishnaraj had prepared a Singaporean meal for us and Baresh spun her beautiful Lazy Susan like a helmsman's wheel to steer a monologue between soy-sauce islands, steamers and dishes from across the world. He seemed to be making up for all those sea nights without the opportunity to gesticulate in front of women. Prins was captivated: he wanted to know all about Bangkok, Hong Kong, Pusan. Anywhere and everywhere. Eventually Mrs K urged us to start eating. Tripti handed out chopsticks. Baresh refused his, 'Fork and spoon, *pliss.*' They would have been like matchsticks in his fingers anyway. But this way he could talk and eat twice as much as the rest of us. Lola hardly ate anything at all; she was addicted to green tea and prawn puffs.

Towards the end of the meal Mira tried to attract Prins's attention with an outrageous story about flying in a biplane across France. But in the middle of it, somewhere over the Loire, Lola shrieked, '*Geese*', and tipped her tea over. Prins quickly dabbed the tablecloth in front of her with his serviette, and then rubbed the front of her blouse with extravagant concern.

Mira was livid. She turned to Baresh of all people. 'So, do you have a joystick on your ship or not?'

o

The moon over the Mersey looked ill the next night, the gas chimneys of Elsemere scorching and reddening it, as we headed back. The flat, newly built motorways were as empty as the moon itself, doodles of an uninterested magician; spellbinding but leading nowhere, riddled with dead ends, unfinished lanes, hard shoulders that gave to gravel, subsoil and passing sand. Ribbons of light and water between the slow hills of the countryside exchanged illumination for stars. Prins drove; I sat next to him. As the needle touched a hundred and ten, I felt a familiar inkling that I have learned to live with now: a sense of accelerating loss for what is behind us – the lost opportunities, the unregainable past – and fear for what lies ahead.

Coming up out of Baresh's cabin, I had remembered how, as a boy, I had first sailed on a ship. I was at that blessed age when I had not yet fully understood the idea of death. To me, then, death was a misfortune. Something that happened only if something went wrong. The ship had a blue funnel. We were anchored in a bay in Trincomalee. A bright sunny day. You could see the hills around the harbour like green elephants slipping in to bathe in the sea. The water was turquoise. I was fishing over the side with a line and a reel. No rod. I would weight the line with lead and swing it out to land like manna for a school of invisible, hopefully hungry, fish. I was not being very successful. The hook kept coming back empty, but I never felt anything like a bite. If I had pulled in a fish, I wouldn't have known what to do. Nevertheless, I was disappointed. Then, as I was squeezing another mound of damp bread around the barb, a Danish deck hand came up to me. 'Any fish down there?' he asked. I didn't know what to say. 'You wait,' he beamed. 'Watch.' He tipped a pail of kitchen scraps over the side of the ship. Within seconds the water was seething with fish. I had never seen anything like it. He let me hold the steering wheel of the motorboat when we all went for a ride around the harbour – then more a nature reserve full of beaches than the harbinger of death it has become. We floated into a small cove. The crew brought out their lager and beautifully canned exotics: frankfurters, olives, cod's roe. But then at the edge of the beach someone discovered the corpse of an old man. It caused a lot of excitement and the outing was abandoned. I heard talk of a natural death. Someone said, 'It happens to us all in the end.' I had never even guessed it before.

I thought such determinism deeply unfair: that fish feed

on garbage, and we feed on fish. That everybody dies. But Prins, speeding along his motorway, betrayed no such feelings; his eyes were trained on the twin beams of his own high-powered Lancia. From time to time he'd take his hand off the wheel and shove Shostakovich or Roxy Music into the tape machine. We hurtled past Frodsham, Runcorn, Knutsford, Birmingham, the road curved like the surface of the globe, hugging the shape of the ground, going down, south, sinking headlong towards the city where some of us will die, little realizing when we first hit the North Circular, Euston or Victoria that there may be no escape; that in ten, twenty, thirty, forty or fifty years there will be the sensation again of the earth rounding, slipping, spinning into its own vortex.

Mira was in the back enveloped in a Nina Ricci mist Baresh had smuggled off the ship for her. She had succumbed to the big man's warm arms soon after the lychee the night before. I heard her goad him, 'Come on, fatso, make me forget what the fuck I'm doing here.' With the two of them in one room, Lola with Prins in the other, and Tripti being otherwise inclined, I felt like the proverbial spare prick at a double-bunk royal bedding.

X

NINE O'CLOCK

Just before the nine o'clock news, Prins peeped in. 'I nodded off,' he complained. 'Damn stupid.'

It was still snowing. It was not a night to go out again.

I offered him a piece of haddock microwaved with Madras paste, the best I could do in the way of home cooking.

'Any news from Naomi?'

I shook my head, still steeped in the oil slicks of the Mersey, trying to connect the tender girl from Manchester briefly cupped in my heart to Lola, the siren, drawing Prins into the bosom of the Vatunases. 'What about Lola?' I asked Prins. 'Did you call her before crashing out?'

'No. It's so complicated.' he grimaced. 'I am crazy about her but that brother of hers, Kia, is dead against me, you know. Not like Dino. And she is so swayed by him. I don't know what the man might have said by now.'

But things seemed to have been going so well for Prins back in Colombo when I met him in '91.

'How often do you get the chance?' he had asked me on his hill-top Shangri-La.

'For a fresh start you mean?'

'No, to dive back in and come up somewhere else. You know, make something new out of something old. Get the best out of both worlds.'

'Never,' I had said. 'You never get that kind of chance. Nobody does.'

He had patted my shoulder, affectionately. 'You are wrong, my friend. You are dead wrong.'

Looking back now I can see how Prins thought the way he did then. His decision to leave London and find a new life in the remains of an old one was proving to have been correct. That was the year Prins had landed a job that he relished in a place that he felt was his; he had found a woman that he loved, who had been the girl next door; he had discovered his father was a paragon in a land of dragons; and, finally, he seemed on the verge of turning blood into wine in a garland of stunning tourist hotels.

o

'Lola loves Kia. They have a strange sibling bond. He seems fond of her too. When he was a boy he only loved music and hunting: high art and fresh air. But after that misadventure, in 1971, Kia never touched a weapon or a record again. He locked himself away and closed his eyes and ears to what was going on in the country. He only re-emerged months later. Then he threw away his hi-fi and his guns and got into spiritualism in a big way. Gurus from here, there and everywhere. Finally, about three years ago, he discovered the Bible. All the other books followed the hi-fi out of the window,' Prins flung out his arm. 'He began to rant on about the sins of the blood, and set to stalking Satan through the jungles of the mind. The only problem is,' Prins clenched his fist, 'the guy doesn't stick to his own head.'

Kia joined one of the new charismatic churches that had started recruiting throughout South and South-East Asia. He became less restless, except when he remembered who he was and the wickedness of the past. 'What the guy can't handle is the fact that the Vatunas wealth, which he still lives off, comes from his so-called devil's temptation that will lead us all to damnation. But who can afford to care about the next world now?' Prins stuck a finger up in the air. 'Before spiritual survival you've got to handle the day-to-day. You gotta live, right? Even his Bibles, they're paying somebody's rent, somewhere, right? It's a business. Maybe on a different planet, but it's the same business. The guru business and the business guru, it's all the same. Dino understands that, why the fuck can't bloody Kia?' Prins stabbed the piece of haddock with his fork.

'Take that exhibition we were planning when I met you in Colombo that time,' Prins placed a hand over half his face, 'what a bloody fiasco. I don't know whether he is mad at me for getting together with Lola, or whether he is insane.' Prins described how Kia had turned up on the last night of the show. 'We had a small party to try and turn a flop into a wake – and he came hunting for Lola.'

'Why paint nipples, for Pete's sake?' Kia had squeaked.

I imagined buttoned-up Lola striding into the foyer, togged up to the neck in flowing silk and with ribbons laced through her hair; prim to her fingernails but bare-breasted with her nipples painted in minute concentric circles of pastel colours and tipped in some leftover psychedelic green. But Prins explained that what had seemed like a canvas teeming with inflated breasts and nipples to Kia was actually a mandala of kinetic space that Lola had recreated in a variety of blues.

'Kia has turned so puritan,' Prins snorted, 'he thinks the only thing that anybody else thinks about is sex. He rushed from canvas to canvas like a fart in a straw hat, sighing. People were milling about for the party, more than had come throughout the whole bloody exhibition.' Prins picked a bone out of the fish on his plate. 'We should have had free booze every night. Or genuine genital-art. A few pieces did get bought that night. Out of curiosity, I guess. People wanted to know what it felt like to buy a painting.' To part with money for no compelling reason and pin their confusion – framed – onto a wall.

'"Why are you letting her show this dirt to people?" Kia demanded. But instead of explaining, I offered him a drink. "A Vambrosia special," I said like an idiot.'

Prins said Kia went ballistic. '"Take it away," he yelped and scampered around the carpet like it was on fire, muttering mantras and covering his eyes.'

Eventually Prins had managed to steer Kia towards the decorative art of another local artist, whose large batiks seemed to adorn almost every five-star hotel in the city. They were ennobling pictures of pastoral life which he thought would soothe the seething fury of Kia's unhinged mind.

'Look,' he had said, 'it is this same style you know. Lola is just concentrating on the dots.'

'You want to humiliate her,' Kia had accused him.

'Dots. Dots, man, can you not see?' Prins had grasped his elbow and pushed him closer to the framed batik. When you get close, he had said, you see nothing but colour and the fundamental circles of our lives.

'I don't want her to suffer so stupidly.'

'She isn't suffering. She is showing her work.'

'She will suffer,' Kia had shaken his hands in front of Prins's face. 'Don't you see? This is not what she needs to do. She needs to open her eyes, you know. And you are not helping her. *You* are making it worse, for you and for her.'

Prins screwed up his eyes in front of me. 'Kia kept repeating "You shouldn't get involved with us. You don't belong here. You don't understand this family and what's been going on here." As if he did. I mean the guy is completely out of his head.'

o

In January, while Pearl was sinking towards her lonely hospital bed, Prins had asked Lola to marry him.

They had gone on a trip together with a couple of photographers who wanted to do yet another book of the island's vanishing wildlife. 'Colombo's coffee tables are now our only libraries, you know,' Prins mocked. 'There are so many exquisite coffee-table books on the *resplendent* island, our *wild* wildlife and our precious quaint Kultur that there's no room even for a fly to fart after breakfast.'

They had booked what he called a 'jungle-bungalow' on the edge of the reserve and gone for the weekend.

'Vasantha, our wildlife man with the telephoto conk, arranged it. He was doing a project with elephants.'

'And you?' I asked.

'Me? I had had an idea, you know. I wanted to come up with a new kind of safari for our hotel business. There'd been all these rumours about the Tigers hiding down there, so I wondered whether I could dream up something. The place is brilliant, you know, for war-watching. If only they can shift the whole combat zone down there. Or maybe, in a few years, someone will dig another hell-hole there. Imagine: camouflage sarongs, sunset flares, Patriot missiles, tracer bullets. You could sit on the veranda and watch the explosions really colour up the sky. Why not? They say that this madness is what we do best, and it's better than the pimping of kids that passes for tourism now.' Despite his sarcasm, Prins's face was sad.

The house is on stilts by a small lake that forms a natural boundary to the game sanctuary. It is private and regularly used only by Vasantha and his friends. But the lake and all its surroundings have been imprinted on the minds of hordes of coffee-table enthusiasts in perfect rectangular shapes with neat, straight borders and the carefully cropped foliage of a thousand photographs. All the creatures of the forest are apparently drawn by the huge lens of the lake, and Vasantha sucks them up through his pneumatic Japanese zoom to recreate them in a pool of silver bromide.

'We were up at the break of day, teacup in one hand, Canon in the other, ready for this jungle of his to spill its beans. Dawn chorus, deer, warthogs all came but no elephant.' Prins said they spent the whole day driving around the lake and even into the reserve itself but all they saw was dung: 'Huge globes of straw-coloured earth dropped from a big anus in the sky. Enough dung to furnish any damn drawing room in the country or outside it, but no creator was anywhere in sight.'

That evening, Prins and Lola had stood on the balcony swiping at giant moths and flying frogs, staring into the moonless black hole of water in the middle of nowhere. Prins suddenly popped the question, like his father's son, shooting for the impossible moonshine. Lola jumped, and spat a flying insect out of her mouth. She said she needed another cigarette. Prins said he lit two cigarettes, like Bogart, and passed one over. They puffed hard to keep away the red devils and said nothing for the rest of the night.

'Next day we gave up the wild-goose chase and went for lunch at the Rest House. But who d'you think we found there?'

'Who?'

'Kia!' Prins slapped his thigh loudly. 'We walk out onto the terrace where they have put the tables for lunch: there are monkeys wanking up the trees, humming birds snorting sugar off the balcony and Kia at a table by himself with a mountain of rice on his plate. His eyes bulge out of his head when he sees us. Me and Lola arm-in-arm like we've come out of Khajuraho, and the other guys behind us with their cameras dangling. His chair falls over backwards. A whine of astonishment peels open his face. "What are you doing here?" he wails.

"Safari," Lola replies. "What do you think?"

'Kia moans. "You can't do this, I told you. There is too much madness in us." Then he turns on the camera buffs who had settled around a table by the balcony rail, near the saucers of sugar water. "You can't go around shooting these pictures. You guys don't know what you are doing. You want the whole world ogling at them?"

'Our Vasantha is really quick. "But we are not killing anyone, men," he retaliates. Kia wheezes and groans and eventually sits back down at his table. One of the servers had put his chair back upright. Kia gulps down his water and glowers like hell at me. "You better watch out too," he warns me. "You are messing with things you don't understand." He acts as if the Vatunases are devils and that somehow he is not one.' Prins huffed, 'But what does he know about anything?'

'You should have asked him,' I said.

'Lola asked him what he was doing there. She was more concerned about him, as usual. Kia said he was looking for a boy – Tivoli's caddie Tito's son – who had not been seen for two weeks. The boy and two of his friends had vanished. The mother was terrified that they might have been "disappeared". "But no one talks if you get out of a Pajero out here," Kia cried, "not even to save their souls." It was as if he had not yet realized how many thousands had been murdered by the fucking squads that overran these last few ghastly years. But . . .' Prins seemed to run out of words.

'And what about the marrying. What did Lola say?'

'She hasn't yet.' Prins looked up, his eyes quickly masking a pattern of secret thoughts. 'Things happened so fast, you know. I haven't had any time with her alone since then.'

'You haven't spoken to her again?'

He rubbed his cheeks, distracted. 'Obviously I did. But marriage is all family stuff, you know. Always a mess.'

XI

MIDNIGHT

'How did she go?' Prins's voice was turning hoarse towards the end of that long day. It was midnight but Prins seemed wide awake after his rest.

I made us two cups of cocoa laced with whisky.

I saw Pearl the night before the night she died. She held my hand so hard that the ring on her finger hurt me. Her fingers were icy. The knuckles had turned white. 'She talked about a tunnel and someone coming,' I felt cold just remembering her words. 'But she looks peaceful now. We can go and see her tomorrow, at the undertakers.'

I couldn't tell Prins much more about the visit. I didn't know how to talk about it. I didn't know what he wanted to hear, and what I wanted to tell. Her death was too recent and Prins too near, then.

It had been a cold day; dark and grey. Never quite

becoming itself before slipping into darkness. Pearl had been in hospital for almost three weeks. The doctor had arranged for her to be taken in after she had complained about palpitations and being short of breath. Perhaps he had suspected cancer. Nobody seemed to know quite what was going on. I walked to the hospital that evening, and back. I needed to move, to feel some mobility, perhaps because she had become so immobile. She had hardly moved for years, but somehow it was different that evening. It was as though if she moved as much as an inch now she would miss something tremendously important coming towards her; and she knew that she should not miss this pulse from somewhere out of this world.

She was propped up in bed, by the window at the end of the ward, more solemn than I was used to. Her face paler than it had been for nearly eighty years, yellowing and drained. She looked better than she had for some time; clearer in shape. Her face seemed to have simplified a lifetime of tribulation into an expression of contentment. But she did not smile when she saw me as she would usually do. She seemed to be looking somewhere else.

I sat down on a vinyl chair next to her bed.

Only later, with my own father's death and my everlasting vigil, would I learn about the chemicals that control the last hours of our lives, the sudden bursts of frenzy, the weird wrestling with inner selves, but at the time I had never been in such a position before. I was not familiar with the signs and signals of a life ending. I assumed an appearance of serenity in a tired face, relaxed by pain killers, was the outward expression of inner peace. I drew connections where none existed. I believed in the possibilities of improvement, continuation, abatement. The inevitability of an end was something I could not yet accept.

Pearl did not look at me at all that evening. She spoke staring straight ahead. 'It's so dark. Like they haven't fixed my eyes.'

I wanted to ask about the halos she used to talk about but I didn't have the courage. I feared something, even though I did not want to think about it.

We spent a long time without words. Longer than I had ever spent in silence with Pearl. Usually the space around her was teeming with words; her whole life was woven with them. But now it seemed all we had was silence.

o

My father also said less and less as his time ran out. You would think he would want to say more, that the approach of death would make you want to say *everything*. But that wasn't the way with him. It was as if he no longer wanted words to work their magic. Better to let go, let go as much as possible. Things, sensations, words, memory. All his life he read books and worked crossword puzzles, then suddenly in the last few days they didn't seem to interest him. But one evening he regained his sense of humour, 'They have no spell any more.' He said it like a child, and smiled at his abandoned crossword.

He had always believed he would die young; a romantic early death. He counted on it and taught himself to live for the present; he never saved for the future. He was always ready to celebrate, rhyme depth with death and let time creep its weary way without his help. But then one day I overheard him say to one of his friends: 'What if I'm wrong? What if we *never* die? That would make a nonsense of everything. All this dancing like it was the last dance.' Perhaps he had been writing his journal – the journal he pretended never to have. Writing, I guess like reading, is about stopping time. Only then do we realize that we do live forever, in a way, as our consciousness rushes in to fill the black hole of a rounded full stop. After that remark I noticed my father would sometimes keep the last two inches of a bottle of Bell's for the next day, or put a bit of *pol-sambol* in the freezer for another meal.

o

When I was about to get up to go, Pearl pulled me back down with her hand. She started speaking again, still looking straight ahead.

'Jason,' she whispered, 'Jason should have known better. He was always such a damn tomfool.'

She spoke as if Jason was next door, not a man from almost forty years ago. A ghost.

Her fingers gripped me hard. They looked brittle: a trap of old bones papered over with a membrane of marbled skin that belied its inner elasticity. There was a strength in them which I would never have suspected. But they were thinner than before; her ring was loose and had turned its stone to her palm. I waited but she said nothing. Her eyes were wide open; she didn't even seem to blink. I waited. I couldn't tell whether she had slipped into a coma. Anything seemed possible. But she was breathing. I could feel a pulse in my hand like a small frog.

A nurse walked by, but didn't seem concerned. I started to get up to call her. But Pearl's fingers tightened around mine. 'Don't go,' she whimpered, '. . . yet.'

I felt then that I might not see her again, alive, after that evening. I did not want to admit it, and I didn't, even later when I was alone. But I think I must have known something was going to happen soon.

Not all our deaths are as vicious or cruel as those who suffer war or famine or the terrors of despots, but the end of a life – even an ordinary life – whether by accident or design, always seems to come too soon to bear. The hurt can never heal. The tears are, perhaps, only our own, but the fault belongs to the whole world.

I thought about Prins and wondered whether I should say something about him to her; whether this was the right moment. She hadn't mentioned him: her only surviving son. Nor Naomi who, though a generation away and already on the brink of bringing forth yet another generation, seemed closest to her. But perhaps at moments like this you go backwards, not forwards, and those who think they have turned the tables on their past and become the guardians of their guardians find the tables turned again and become powerless once more. Perhaps you go back to all those things from which you thought you had escaped. As though, just when you think you are in control, you lose control. The father you buried, the mother you tamed, suddenly reappear as they were at the beginning of life. If you are lucky, perhaps this is the best thing that could happen; but if those early years were a torment, then maybe there is a hell not of your own making yet to come.

'I was lucky in my birth,' she breathed hard, 'but with Jason I was blind. It ran out too early. And God help me, I know I need it now. Luck.' Her eyes swivelled, as if unsure which way to look. Then she closed them and lowered her head. She rested her face on herself.

The lights were bright in the ward but outside it was dark. So very dark. I could see myself walking home in the darkness, but I couldn't imagine Pearl going anywhere. The imagination, I know, likes an easy ride: familiar territory, landmarks, toeholds and handgrips. A true life.

Pearl seemed to read my mind. 'I never imagined it would be like this.'

'What?'

She didn't explain. Instead she started breathing more noisily, more deliberately.

I had brought her some strawberries; I couldn't find the cherries she loved anywhere. It was one of those rare fruits that seemed not to belong to the global market and be ever present everywhere. I thought strawberries would be the best alternative. But she didn't touch them. Maybe I should have gone for plums. Dark purple plums with the glow of a southern sun hidden in them; flesh that might give her light, inside.

From time to time she would squeeze my hand harder as if trying to lift herself, using me as a walking stick. I couldn't tell whether she was trying to reach somewhere – into her tunnel? Away from her tunnel? Or whether she was simply readjusting her sore body.

'Does it hurt?' I asked stupidly.

She shook her head. But I knew that she had been in pain for many years. She was not one who complained of pain, although she would often talk of her collapsing bones and disintegrating body as if it were a house no one cared to live in any more. Perhaps she meant there was no new pain, or perhaps it was under control in her hospital bed. Perhaps it didn't matter any more.

○

Prins took another sip of cocoa. I poured more whisky into his mug, and then mine. There were still lumps of cocoa powder floating on the top. If crushed they would burst open and spill dry powder that had been protected from the hot water by a skin of wet grains.

'Yes, she went quietly,' I added to my reply about her departure.

'I don't know whether I wish I had been here, or not,' Prins spoke slowly. 'There would have been so much to untangle, we'd never have done it. It would have been so . . . unresolved.'

There was nothing he could do about it now. But he looked as though it hurt him to admit the gulf between his life and hers. I found it difficult, at the time, to recall the mother he would have remembered; but for him it was now impossible to ever know the Pearl I had got to know.

Over the twelve years he had been away she had aged imperceptibly to those around her, but hugely to those who knew her only from before.

'There are some so simple things that need to be said and when it's too late to say them, then it becomes almost unbearable.' Prins winced as he sipped his warm whisky.

Pearl said something very similar to me once. She said, 'There are so many more stories I wish I had told, you know. I am an old lady with a lot of untold tales.'

'So tell them,' I urged. 'Tell them now.'

'You can't *just* tell them. You should know. It has to be the right time and the right place. They tell themselves, if you are lucky.'

'When *is* the right time, then?'

'I should have started years ago. Before he went. While he was still willing to stay in the room.'

'Prins?'

She sighed. 'But he could never understand. Like Ravi, even Anoja. Like Jason, I suppose.'

I waited for her to talk some more. Pearl was someone who liked to talk: she had always taken great pleasure in the movement of her mouth, in making sounds, in stringing syllables together, words, sentences, in giving shape to her thoughts and the perpetual crackling across the canyons of her brain, in making patterns for the rest of us. On her sofa in her yellow room she broadcast her whole inner life with the immortal cackle of a ripe pun. While some people are dumbfounded by TV, and retreat into solipsistic mind-games, Pearl found the low-level radiation of the TV screen a wonderful sounding board for her own output. She could *talk*. It was a trait she had passed on to Prins but withheld from both Ravi and Anoja. It had re-emerged again only in Naomi.

But on these last few occasions I could see that talking had by then become almost too much of an effort. It was not like those extraordinary afternoons when her stories would carry me far beyond the electronic images of her glowing box into a boundless world of breath where all of our histories would bend like light to suit our daily survival.

She paused for an incredible two minutes – absolute silence – before continuing. 'Everything became so difficult after Ravi was born. That house was driving me mad.'

'Arcadia?'

'Anything but . . .' she grimaced. 'None of them ever understood, *putha*, what it was really like. How could they? Babies. They are just babies.'

Pearl sometimes liked to draw circles around us with her talk. Slowly to bind her audience to a world of her own making; make it so that nothing else existed, at least for the moment. She liked to mystify and to entrance, but on this occasion I think she was genuinely unable to say anything more about the slowly atrophying convolutions of her imagined life. She looked at me as if from a great distance.

'But at least you were here to hear me out, no? I am thankful for that.' Then she chuckled, 'And I'll go before I'm too decrepit to cut my own toenails. Who would do that for me otherwise? Not you, *putha*, not you.'

Although she could still make me laugh, I found it very difficult to be with her in the hospital. It seems unfair that we didn't know she was approaching the end so fast. And yet it is so obvious now that her life, hour by hour, was drawing to a close. It was almost written on her face. A darkening around the mouth, shadows around the eyes, a smoothening of the skin as though a thousand worry lines were subsiding into one great fault line that would soon crack the heart beneath the surface forever. But, at the time, no one ever really believes that an end can be so near. You only sense difficulties, frustrations, and your own instinct to push away the darkness and make believe there is light – light everywhere. You can't see the fleshless segments of a disappearing universe.

Prins never had to contend with this. His father's death was nothing more than a story, something that existed in newspaper reports and unreliable anecdotes. His own memory of the time seemed not to exist; he was shielded from the whole business. He wasn't there. And when Anoja and Ravi went, he was already well out of their lives. Now he was mercifully excluded from his mother's death, although he would say mercy is only ever yours.

Prins put down his mug and stretched out his fingers. This time he said, 'It's all always in your own hands, isn't it?'

'What?'

'Fate. The chance to be free. How we choose to live.'

I was not so sure. I wished it was all up to ourselves, but sometimes I felt too powerless. I tried to tell Prins what his mother had said about him. The difficulties of those early years of his infancy, his father's demise and their leaving of Arcadia. Her desire to speak to him; her feeling that it was never the right time. But I found my own words missing bits, closing gaps, papering over the cracks. It was not the right time, and now it seems it never can be.

He listened to me. Occasionally his eyebrows would move, or he would pull at his lower lip. Eventually he said, 'She knew something, didn't she? But she didn't want to say. She didn't want me to know. Somehow I think it's all connected, but she has buried it now.'

In all the years I had known Prins I had never seen any real sign of regret in him. He was a man who looked firmly ahead even when he was going round in circles. When he looked back it was usually only to measure how far he had come. But that night, when he spoke of burying Pearl, his eyes were streaming, pierced by the chill of the past.

'I scarpered out of here, you know, for a damn good reason. Not just for puttering about. I wanted out of the tangled-up life we had here. The confusion of being nowhere. It made no sense, and I wanted to get a real life. Find something that would make sense of my life. But I think I ended up going straight back into a bigger bloody mess.'

o

When Pearl went, she went on her own, just as she had wanted to. In the end she seemed to know what it was she wanted, what she could not ever have, and what she needed. There was no one left to be with her: I suppose I was not really the right person and Naomi was taking care of a new life. Anoja, Jason, Ravi were all on the other side of the great divide – and Prins was on the other side of the world.

Dylan was the last of us to see her alive and the first to see her dead. The one who knew her least but last. It would be just like her to make the point that none of us knew much of anything, and so little of her.

Naomi called me on the telephone and said, 'She's gone.'

I wasn't ready for it. 'What?'

'She's gone.'

'Who?' I wasn't thinking.

When she told me it was Pearl I was struck dumb. I knew it had to happen, but I had not been there that night; I had visited the night before. Dylan and I were taking it in turns. I was going to go again that evening. I wished I had been there two nights in a row. We all knew she didn't have long but I had hoped there would be, at least, a few months. Long, slow months and then an imperceptible change in the world that we knew. It didn't happen that way then, and it didn't happen that way later with others in my life. Maybe we are all always taken by surprise.

Naomi said that she did not know who else to call. Dylan was at the hospital. I was the only other person she had talked to. She had tried to speak to Prins, at his bungalow by Shangri-La, but there had been no answer. 'Where could he be?'

'Anywhere,' I said. I did not know then that he had already moved back to Colombo.

'But nobody answered. There should be somebody in the house. Are you sure you gave me the right number?'

I suggested she send a fax to his head office.

'There's nobody else to call,' Naomi almost whispered down the line. 'It's so weird.'

I could only think of Baresh, but he could be bobbing around anywhere in the world.

Pearl was more alone than I had ever realized. Her network had vanished over time. Or perhaps it had been slowly, patiently, clipped away.

'Pearl with no oyster for a shell,' she used to sing, warming a pan of butter rice, the geyser gurgling in the background like the sea outside her first childhood home.

Somehow I had imagined her life was more crowded, that there was more going on than visits from Naomi and Dylan and me in her daily life. That somehow all the people of her past were constantly moving in and out of her sitting room. That she was in touch with everything and everyone all the time. Instead it seems we were all she had besides the brushlight of the TV screen, disembodied voices on the radio and junk mail. Where were the figures from her past? The Ishranis? The Sanderson Bros. pensioners? The people from those early years in London? Were they all only in her head, evaporated ghosts in the ether of our collective memory like Iain and Tivoli? Like Ravi and Anoja and Jason?

o

Pearl might have outlived many of her generation – defined in terms of those who started out with her – her forgotten schoolmates, her neighbours, those anonymous shadows around her father's many airy houses, and those more closely linked to the borders of Arcadia. But everywhere there are others who have floated longer, some happier, some less so, and the innumerable ones who vanish younger and younger with apparently increasing brutality all over the world. But her death, that cold winter, was the closest I had experienced then. It made me aware for the first time of the density of what surrounds us, the transformations that take place in our lives, the capricious acts of disappearance performed every day.

Sometimes it seems we are cocooned in a skin of time which, if ruptured, lets life slip out to disappear forever. Our repairs, it seems, can only be made out of hope when the skin is drawn tighter. Ravi slipped out of a hole in my world I did not even know existed. Others have fallen through it, but I never noticed the frayed edges until it ripped wide open with Pearl going, and since then it seems to keep getting bigger however hard I try to fix it. After my father, now I know, one day, I will fall through it myself.

o

Prins and I had got through the best part of a bottle of Bell's, with cocoa and without cocoa, by one-thirty in the morning. I felt rooted; Prins uprooted. I think he already knew something of the shape of things to come although he did not want to talk about it. All day he had been play-ing with the past but only going so far, feeding me a line, playing it out, reeling it in, but not going to the edge of what he knew even then. I still do not know whether this was because of his own fears, or whether he found me now a constraint rather than the release I used to be. Within a day it seemed we had traversed too many lifetimes. From being a revealer, he was suddenly, in the middle of the night, turning into a secret.

I suggested we call it a day. Sleep might help. The next morning we could try Naomi again and pick up the rest of the story. I had also promised to take him to the funeral parlour.

Prins blew out a loud breath of frustration. He slammed his fist into his other hand. 'You know, nothing really fits. That's the trouble. It all pretends to fit, like someone has constructed it all for us to see exactly how the thing works, but really it is done to hide everything. To lead us completely in the wrong direction. I feel I have been given a puzzle with a ready-made solution to divert me from something else which I must not discover. The watch on the beach doesn't work. Never did. It's a fake. Therefore the God who made it is a fake. D'you know what I mean?'

Prins, that night, seemed on the verge of discovering, or perhaps revealing, what lay behind the veils of our ordinary lives; but there seemed to be a step he could not take, or would not take, yet.

XII

DAWN

At two minutes past seven the next morning the telephone rang. I was awake, nursing a cup of tea in my bed. I picked up the receiver, 'Hullo?'

'It's a girl,' a voice trembled in my ear. 'A girl.'

It took me a moment to work out that it was Dylan. I had trouble responding. The whole world seemed silent. Everything seemed silent. 'Congratulations!' I said eventually. 'How's Naomi?'

'Mother and daughter are fine, both fine,' he replied proudly down the line.

'Where are you?' I felt that deep familiar need for orientation.

'In the hospital. I just came out of the theatre.'

'Prins is here,' I said. 'We've been looking for you and Naomi.'

'She'll be thrilled,' his throat seemed dry, the melodious voice choked. 'Wonderful.'

Thrilled with the baby, sure; but Prins? 'A girl?' I said for want of anything else and sensing Dylan's need to go over his excitement again.

'Yeah. Eight pounds and ten ounces. A big girl.'

I asked whether he had been in the hospital all night.

'Since yesterday,' he made it sound like a poem. 'I think it was yesterday morning. It's like it's been forever.'

'A lifetime?' I was breaking into the day, my brain slowly unlocking, shivering down its sleep-fattened dendrites. But he was too tired to catch it. 'So what happens now.'

'They rest, I guess. The nurse told me I should come back later. One of your Lankan girls, the nurse. Shoba. Wonderful.'

I told Dylan to come over and have some breakfast.

'I'll see what's going on first. She's wonderful. I'll be over soon.'

Outside, the silence of freshly fallen snow pressed against the window panes; there was no traffic to be heard on the roads. This was silence like the dream of heaven. I began to realize how wrong all those composers were who heaped scales upon scales in their vain attempts to capture the grandeur of heaven: what they really needed to do was to stop. To hold their breath and try to imagine a stilled heart and the peace that can only come from the absence of conflict, of abrasion, of friction, of sound itself. No wonder we never hear the angels on our shoulders: they do not speak. They melt at the prospect of sound, perhaps even prayer. Heaven is not music: heaven, if anything, must be silence. The stillness of the centre, the eye of a storm whirling across the universe. An unveiling mind.

When our breath is finally released tongueless, like a soul from the trappings of the body, there can only be silence.

Prins had claimed, the night before, that there was a difference of four ounces between the weight of a dead body and a living one. A body with breath and without. The weight of a silent soul, I reckon, freed from the roar of life.

But by eight o'clock I was downstairs making my small chirrup towards our communal existence: toaster crackling, kettle steaming, eggs bubbling and bacon sizzling just like Pearl's kitchen in 1975, where I had learned to greet a London day through a haze of unrefined cholesterol. I turned over my glass egg-timer.

When I opened the curtains I saw snow falling again in that absurd cross-hatched fashion I have never got used to. I watched the endless stream of white flakes pouring down: first slanting one way, then the other, and then, confused by some gust of wind, sideways or in an upward swirl, before turning back into a steady straight fall like sand in a glass tube.

Prins once said that someone somewhere is meticulously plotting the behaviour of crowds and developing a theory that will predict the startling dive of a school of herring, the ripple of abuse in a stadium, the fall of sand into perfect heaps or the dash and verve of shoppers sniffing bargains in a Singapore megastore. Would it work for snowflakes too? By moving in a crowd and drawing patterns in the air, do they too take on some kind of abstract notion of consciousness that comes from acting as an entity: becoming a law in itself and therefore a lawmaker? Another level of being? God knows, we need it. The second law of thermodynamics is not good enough. Somewhere things must group together sometime. They *must*. The hospital is about two miles from the kitchen window. Not in view but close enough to imagine the walk there, every step of the way. In it there are perhaps a thousand beds filled by the infirm, the daily wounded of an ordinary late-twentieth-century city brought to adjoining beds of hope and hopelessness. In one wing Pearl had lain for her last few days occasionally shuffling from TV room to toilet, when the going was good, but mostly slipping from one painful memory to another as her hold loosened on the things around her. And now, a few yards away, beyond a wall, a corridor and a few tubs of linen and lint, lay Naomi with her new-born baby.

The day before Prins turned up I was stopped by a woman in a green duffel coat. 'Are you going to the bakery?' she asked. I nodded gravely over the lip of my zipped-up leather jacket. She said, 'It's closed. Don't bother, it's closed today.' But it never closes, I thought. It has *never* been closed when I have gone there. Always there are pastries crumbling on the shelves, baguettes keeling over, and stuffed pancakes in slow petrification, Bath buns, Chelsea buns and Eccles cakes like in a fifties film. But why should she lie? The woman turned and walked away, heading for the Baptist church hall. I felt the need for the future to hold something. Anything. For it to hold. For it not to give way completely. We need to believe that things will work out, that tonight we will sleep and tomorrow wake up. And that tomorrow, we will remember today. What we did today, what happened yesterday – and have some faith in what will happen tomorrow. Some tendency towards order. I had a green duffel coat once with toggles like a boar's teeth and a hood that seemed to trap the coldest air. I bought it on Pearl's advice for my first winter.

Before the eggs were ready, Prins stumbled down.

'Did I wake you?' I asked. I had been banging the cupboard doors looking for the bread knife.

Prins yawned sleepily and then started at the sight of the pile of snow on the kitchen window sill.

'Hey, you are a *great*-uncle today.' I told him the news.

'A girl, huh?' He stretched back like a big-time movie-screen executive. 'I dreamed of my mother. She had just been asleep. She got out of a cardboard coffin and came here to wake us up. It was a big joke for her. She was giggling like a little girl.' Prins looked at me as if for corroboration.

'Dylan will come over for breakfast. Afterwards we can go and see them, I guess.'

I got some more bacon out of the fridge. I put the already cooked bacon in a dish in the oven and put the new bacon under the grill. Somewhere in the cellar, probably behind the disintegrating stack of old punctured tyres, I knew I had a bottle of cheap Hungarian champagne I had picked up in Budapest. I went to look for it. 'Keep an eye on the bacon,' I said to Prins. We needed to celebrate, I thought. I wanted to be busy. Pearl would have wanted us to celebrate; there is time enough for mourning in the rest of our lives. The moment to celebrate comes less often, it seems, and must be grasped before it too becomes melancholic.

The cellar was brimming with junk. I found the bottle in the well of a dead VW wheel, as I had suspected. It was cold. The doorbell rang while I was still rummaging, seized by a need to find a screwdriver I had once lost down there.

Prins opened the door just as I came up the stairs. Dylan was on the front steps with snow in his hair, his round face glowing pink like the sun.

'Prins, hello.'

'Hallo,' Prins said, not quite knowing what to make of

Dylan, or how to greet a stranger who was also family. They had never met before, although Dylan had seen pictures of Prins.

I shouted out my congratulations and popped the cork. Prins jumped as if he had been shot. He had become nervous again, like at the fire the day before.

'Champagne,' I announced and rushed for the tumblers on the breakfast table. I poured a glass while Dylan hung up his coat.

'So? Are they OK?' I gave him a glass.

'Fine. They are both fine. Sleeping. I came straight here.' He stood like a bear with a glass in his paw.

I poured another one for Prins. 'Cheers, here's to the newest!'

Dylan sat down and blurted out his story of waters breaking, the rush to the hospital, labour wards, epidurals, operating theatres and surgical masks. An emergency Caesarean. A jumble of information and technicalities about entering this world that seemed to have exhilarated and overwhelmed him. Prins and I listened in a world of our own, eating bacon and eggs and sipping bubbly wine.

'You look more jet-lagged than Prins,' I said.

Dylan grinned, his eyes glazed.

O

Half a jar of marmalade disappeared at that breakfast. Three men, a jar of marmalade, a carton of broken eggs, a thick-lipped bottle of fizzy Chardonnay: the still life of a new Cézanne.

As the bubbles subsided, our conversation collapsed. Dylan buttered his toast while Prins sipped his wine, coffee and orange juice in quick succession.

'Should we go see her – them – today? Is it allowed?' I asked. Birth, like death, seemed an out-of-bounds affair. A dimension with its own rules and laws; customs we were unaccustomed to. Neat demarcations that are eroding fast – for me.

Dylan looked up. 'Maybe you can come later. About four.'

Then silence grew over us. The silence of men who, after their excitement, want to be left alone. To do nothing but follow a well-worn circuit leading nowhere. A nervous system that requires routine, order, quiet ordinary functioning, a flossed head and a clean rectum. Somehow to keep the pretence that nothing has changed, all is well. We are creatures who need games with familiar rules. No surprises. May the Lord protect us from surprises. Near-surprises are acceptable, as long as the resolution follows a known pattern. We need to know the shape of the end, so that it is recognized when reached. Every book needs its last page, only the heart needs more.

Dylan stared down at his plate but his mind seemed somewhere else, perhaps investigating with the tip of his purple veined tongue the sugary nooks and sand crannies of a set of deformed teeth. Eventually it was he who spoke. 'Dawn,' he ran his tongue around his mouth. 'We are calling her Dawn.' He was the father at the table.

Prins opened his eyes and looked at him as if he had said something deeply profound. 'Dawn,' he repeated the name – the word – like a prayer.

o

The small patch of grass that was my garden was obliterated by the snow. It lay like a dollop of thick cream. But day had broken through with a gilt brush. Everything shone. The kitchen window was finely veined with rivulets of dust and grime, a vertically suspended solution of the world's smallest grains, frozen as if by the momentary sleep of time. I wanted so much for this to be the beginning of something new in the world. For that winter eye in the sky to burn away past failures and let something pristine, uncontaminated, innocent burst free. But the pulse of hope itself made me sink into the body I inhabited. Flesh consuming flesh, growing heavier and heavier, creating its own gravity, pulling back each thought until one day nothing will be able to escape the clutches of the self. In the end, it seems, we will be nothing but another collapsing spark in a burnt-out, spinning sky.

○

Later in the day I took Prins to the funeral parlour. I left him alone to see his mother. The shell that remained.

When he came out of her cold room, he said nothing.

○

In her hospital bed, Naomi looked exhausted. She appeared all flat, like a piece of paper laid out on a mattress with only the head still remaining round, full and pregnant. A tiny baby was sucking the little remaining energy out of her. Prins stood by the bed, his big ram's head bowed and his eyes like glass catching the yellow light bouncing from the snowy hills outside and holding it melting inside.

'You came back,' Naomi whispered. She had thought he

would never come as there had been no response to her faxes telling him of Pearl's death and then, a couple of days later, the garbled details of the funeral.

Prins shrugged.

The baby had fallen asleep with her mouth open.

'She reminds me . . .' he paused. The baby's sleeping face, the unstretched skin and newly formed features still finding their proportions in the unconfined air, seemed to merge into the shape of a face at the other end of life: Pearl's slowly collapsing face, the features subsiding into her over-extended skin. A story, rich as blood, riding her veins to mark the pages of her own book; the first page here in an indecipherable face and the last page somewhere that, when it comes, will seem after our initial surprise, to be precisely where we had expected without ever quite realizing it. But this was a baby with luck in her eyes, the sad blood of the past perhaps finally thinned out three generations on.

We sat together for a while collecting our thoughts, gathering strength from each other's presence, from the baby, and letting the world spin in each of our heads, the blood's pulse renewing it time and again. For how long?

'He's done all the arrangements for tomorrow,' Naomi told Prins, touching me. 'All the paperwork . . . everything.'

'With Dylan,' I added.

Naomi had asked me to help with the funeral; I had no idea of what to do. I had never dealt with death before and although Naomi had been around when Ravi died, she had not been able to take in any of the practicalities. We had no one of our own with experience to hand. We took everything step by step, choosing the easiest option at each stage: cremation, a plain urn, the simplest service. Dylan brought the catalogue home for Naomi to choose a coffin. 'I can't,' she cried and flung it far from the pile of baby brochures on the sofa. In the end Dylan and I had to decide.

'But we don't know what to do about hymns, or psalms. Nothing seems right.' There wasn't even a poem that came close to the emptiness we felt. 'Will you tell the vicar something today?' Naomi asked Prins.

He nodded, wordlessly.

Naomi had an old glass clock on the table next to her bed. It was about the size of a pocket camera and shaped like a shell. The clock face was set into the middle.

'Her clock? You brought her clock?' Prins stared at it.

'She gave it to me when I got pregnant. You know how I hate to wear a watch.'

It was a beautifully moulded piece of glass. I picked it up. There was the number 1953 and an ornate inscription on the back. I read it out, 'An oyster for a shell, love T.'

'J,' said Prins. 'It's a J. For Jason.'

'No,' Naomi looked puzzled. 'It wasn't written for her, was it?' The baby began to cry. A tiny cry, the sound of a voice finding air.

○

The funeral, the next day, was a modest occasion. Prins had called the vicar after we got back from the maternity ward, and asked for silence. Nothing else. Pearl would have understood. She had no more words for us.

In the morning, Prins and I went straight to the crematorium together. There was no need for a cortège. Prins was in his new black clothes, but even more bleary-eyed than the day before. Naomi was still at the hospital with the baby. Dylan said that she had tried to come but was too breathless; tears had been streaming down her face. They had put her back on a drip. Dawn had salt, as well as milk, on her first new day. There was nothing we could do about Naomi. The funeral could not be postponed, even though we were the only ones who were going to be there. 'Naomi can do something when the ashes are buried,' Prins suggested, 'or scattered in the garden of souls.' Pearl would have wanted them scattered in the sea, I thought, surely never on land.

262

DAWN

Pearl came to the crematorium in a hearse grander than anything she had been in since Ravi died. Prins, Dylan and I, together with three strangers from the funeral parlour, carried the rosewood coffin in. We were too close to each other and had to shuffle; it weighed a ton. As we tottered up the aisle I thought we would collapse at the altar and Pearl would end up crushing Prins in a last absurd prank. But we managed to ease the sleek, surprisingly slim, box down onto the rollers without mishap. Prins placed a heap of pink carnations on top and staggered down to the front pew. The anonymous chapel was constructed out of the barest essentials: grey brick walls enclosing a cold space, oblivious to the coming and going of mourners and the transformation of the dead from flesh to ash. Our congregation must have been one of the smallest and quietest: a silent coffin, the three of us, and the handful of those whose job it was to be there.

That day I felt Pearl was leading us down an ever quietening road that had darkened with the death of her mother, whom she never spoke about, then her father, and then had grown even darker with the passing of Jason, Anoja, Ravi and finally herself. In the silence I wondered whether when we died, Prins or I, would we be in a deeper silence of an even more fractured world? I imagined Lola, Mira, Tripti, Baresh and others from our past reappearing as old women and men with brittle bones and failing memories determined to give their lives, and ours, a hint of depth: of something beyond the petty anxieties and mean tribulations of our rambling days.

o

When we stepped outside I found a line of cars parked gingerly next to the deck of old graves, their wheels rubbing against the sloping shoulders of the snow-heaped kerb, and streaks of salt in the tarmac like the shadows of the departed smudged into the road.

A few yards away a crowd had gathered in the cold. They were there to mourn the passing of someone we knew nothing about. The clouds above were speckled with mushroom dust as if slightly mouldy, or as though they had caught the sad soot from the chimney that delivered the mortal to a metaphorical heaven.

o

After the funeral, Prins went on his own to see Naomi again. He told me later that she couldn't stop crying. She had given him Pearl's silver ring which I had retrieved from the undertaker's and passed on.

I picked him up from the hospital and took him to Pearl's flat. He had only a few hours left before his flight.

Prins looked around the place like a professional surveyor – taking in the old dark furniture, the bits and pieces, her TV, the streaky windows lined with black mould, the fuzzy view of a snowed-in garden. 'With a new baby to deal with they'll never have the time to clear this place out.' He blinked.

I offered to do it. I knew that I wanted to be there alone for a while, to sit on the old cracked leatherette chair and remember her as she was.

There wasn't that much left to do. In the last couple of months, after Naomi moved out, Pearl had been bagging a lot of the old junk in black bin liners and feeding it to the yellow council vulture that steamed by every Thursday morning. Perhaps learning something from her younger son, Ravi. In her bedroom we discovered an old suitcase crammed with Prins's old winter clothes, and parcels of brittle paper. 'This can all go,' he cleared his throat loudly and snapped the locks shut. Only the kitchen seemed to be as cluttered as ever with things whose significance were lost forever with the passing of their owner.

Then behind the sofa, in the sitting room, I found her knitting basket with an unfinished yellow baby cardigan, her knitting needles and a heap of fluffy wool. She hadn't taken it to hospital. Under the wool was a big, square biscuit tin. The lid was buckled and didn't quite fit. A couple of strips of old tape had come unstuck along the edge, but a cross of grey twine held it in place. The label over the border of brown and black dots masquerading as autumn flowers read '1936–66', in her spidery handwriting.

Prins picked it up. He took it over to the dining table and sat down. Slowly he undid the string and prised open the lid. Packets of folded paper had been jammed into a pile of small, blue notebooks. He lifted one up and hesitated for a moment. I stared at it, trying to make out the writing on the cover. But then he quickly stuffed it back in unopened.

'Whose are the notebooks?' I asked. I couldn't imagine Pearl writing in such neat notebooks. 'Don't you want to look?'

Prins fitted the lid back on and carefully retied the string around the tin. He took a deep breath. 'I can't any more. I know too much already. I don't want to discover another damn thing.' He smoothed down one of the pieces of tape on the lid; his eyes were red and flickering. I thought of his mother's graceful candle flames. Their perfect shape. The promise of everlasting flame. Prins seemed to shrink back as if to retreat from his parents' past, his past. He closed his eyes. 'I loved her,' he said softly. His fingers were trembling.

But I reminded him that he was the one who wanted to

pick at the entrails, who wanted to find out how it had all begun. He was the one who thought that Jason Ducal was murdered by his enemies and not the accidental victim of somebody else's suicide attempt. Here was a chance to throw some light on those early years.

'Who cares anyway?' Prins angrily pushed the tin away and glared at me. 'I *know* there were two bullets fired the night he died. One for each of them. But only one ever got into the official reports. The other was recovered. It was murder, and it was fixed. I am sure of that. But who cares any more? Now they are both gone, it's a dead world. There is enough bloody trouble in the one we live in, you know.'

I didn't understand what he meant; what could be more important, I wanted to ask. But even as the words formed in my head, I realized I couldn't utter them. Prins was adjusting his world the only way he could, just as I was mine.

In the end, he calmed down and asked me to dispose of Pearl's precious biscuit tin for him. 'Let the kids be free of all this,' he said, meaning Naomi and her daughter. 'It's a bomb, sitting there, ticking like that bloody clock.' He tapped his fingers against his mouth, echoing one of Pearl's gestures. 'Chuck it out, will you, just chuck the whole lot out. There was a lot more to her than this stuff . . .'

But I couldn't. There was hardly anything else left. Only that one tin box packed with words. The sheets of paper freighted with ink were the only tangible bits left to anchor the stories she used to entrance me with as we sipped our sherry together and imagined another world for ourselves. I had to keep the biscuit tin – its contents distilled, as it were, over six decades.

The blue notebooks turned out to be Jason's schoolmasterly journals covering his life with Pearl in increasing detail right up to his last night, and the heap of folded paper was Pearl's own sporadic outbursts marking the thirty years from her marriage until Prins came to live with her in London after Anoja died. At the bottom of the tin I found bundles of letters from her children when they were young, from her admirer T – Tivoli, it had to be – and from Jason in the early years. Each telling its own special story and hiding another between every line.

I kept the tin and its heap of tiny philosopher's stones ostensibly for Pearl. In her memory. But now I know I really kept it for me: for me to dig my hands in and feel her life slip through my fingers, again and again.

o

After I had cleared the rest of the flat, I wrote to Prins to tell him that it was all done. I also told him that the biscuit tin was the one thing I could not throw away. 'I've kept it,' I wrote, 'the blue notebooks contain your father's last words.' I didn't mention the letters.

I didn't mention anything at all about the biscuit tin or its contents to Naomi and Dylan. They were on the verge of moving out of my life as well. When her maternity leave ended Naomi was expected to relocate, with the rest of her colleagues, to Manchester; it seemed like a good move.

About six weeks after I posted my letter to Prins, a parcel arrived for me from Colombo with writing like a spider's web on it. Enclosed in it was a thick, Alwych journal with a weatherproof black cover. A folded newspaper clipping was fastened to the front. The clipping showed a photograph of Dino Vatunas, President of the newly formed Great Sands Corporation, standing proud at his brother Kia's funeral. The article below explained that Kia Vatunas had died in a bomb explosion outside his house. There was one other casualty: one Mohan Jayasuriya, a former journalist. Prins had scribbled on the margin: 'You might as well keep mine too. I have to get the hell out of this hole. P.' The journal was crammed with Prins's jottings about the Ducals and all the Vatunases coiled around them. Ten years of tiny entries increasing in frequency as he tried to preserve some vision of hope in a descent into mayhem. Here was a whole history of misfortune, captured in his laconic writing.

I remembered seeing the journal in his hands that night when he spread out the articles about Jason's death on my pine table. He didn't open it then, but I could see now that it must have been only two-thirds full at the time. The last forty pages had all been filled since Pearl's funeral. These were pages where the writing was fast and big:

Monday 22/2/93: Disaster. Dino knows every move I make. Shouldn't have gone to the meeting in such a state.

Friday 26/2/93: What is she so frightened of? She won't talk. She says Kia will tell me. Lola is *too too* complicated.

Saturday 20/3/93: Message from Mohan J. Wants to meet at Galle Face Hotel day after tomorrow. Joker cadging another drink.
Must talk to Dino again.

Monday 22/3/93: No bloody Mohan!

The very first page of the journal had been written about a year and a half after he first arrived in Colombo and was, by contrast, neat and measured.

DAWN

Sunday 3 April 1983 (Ravi's birthday)

Earlier this evening I took a walk by Arcadia. Dusk.
The mosquitoes were rising. The house was in shadow.
The foxbats had started to fly. They came out of the
trees behind Bellevue in their hundreds and passed over
Arcadia. A line of ghouls flapping their oilskin shrouds
and heading God knows where. Why do they fly so
mournfully?

I telephoned Prins from London the same evening I received
the parcel, but there was no answer. The next day I called his
office in Colombo but was told by his secretary that he was
away on business. A day later I was told he was no longer in
the business. I found Lola's number and tried her. 'He's
gone, everything is going,' she mumbled, barely acknowl-
edging me, and hung up in a crackle of loose wires. Nobody
else I spoke to knew anything of his whereabouts. Perhaps
he had really run away again: this time, like Ravi, erasing
his exit lines. Prins, it seemed, like all the Ducals, had gone.

o

When I left London on my trip to Japan, a few days later, I

271

didn't realize that thereafter I would be perpetually on the road, retracing the footsteps of the past. Always hoping to find, I guess, something that would make sense out of the nonsense of my life: the alchemist's dream. I know how to live with only a modem and a slip of plastic, but with each jolt I find I yearn for a story without an end.

Every night I dream of the furnace of death, the dry blistering heat of breath that escapes the body never to return, the numbing coldness of a room bereft. It is only a glitch of nature, I know, but I can't free myself. When I wake up I feel swollen, thirsty, stupidly powerless.

LATER

The day I reached Colombo, on my stopover back from Tokyo, the leading opponent of the Government was assassinated at a political rally. Within a week, on the eve of my departure, a May Day blast blew up the President of the country in front of television cameras. The whole place was in turmoil. Rumours were rife and everybody had their own savage story to tell of horror and brutality from the present and the past.

I didn't know where to start looking for Prins. His former office seemed a dead end and I couldn't get hold of Lola again. I tried The Cool Kurumba, that he had mentioned, but no one seemed to know him there. Then that evening, in my hotel lobby, I bumped into a group of his drinking partners that I had met on my previous visit. I asked about Prins, but no one seemed very concerned.

'Bugger must have hooked it with all these bloody bombs bursting all over the place,' one chortled.

'When you find him, tell the fellow he owes me five thousand bucks.'

'Damn fool poked around too much with those Vatunases, you know.'

'Talk to Lola, *men*. That's the girl,' the man I recognized as Vasantha, the photographer, suggested. He said that she was staying over at Mira's house on the other side of town.

I had not thought of Mira; I had assumed she was somewhere else with her wealthy husband.

I hardly recognized Lola when I saw her. She had cut her hair short; her face was puffed up, her eyes strained with tears. She didn't say anything when she saw me. I held her hands in both of mine and tried to get her to talk. I could feel the knob of a ring against the palm of my right hand. She was wearing Pearl's ring.

Her voice was even fainter than before. 'Prins said we could live in his old house,' she murmured. 'He promised to arrange everything. But then he went out one evening to Liberty Plaza, or somewhere, to buy a bulb for his car and didn't come back. I've waited and waited, but he hasn't come back. Now there's nothing left. I don't know when he'll come back.'

I asked her, 'When did he go?'

She remembered my telephone call from London. 'It was the day before you called,' she whimpered.

'Have you checked with the police?' I asked, and then felt foolish when I saw the tears well up in her eyes.

'I called Mira,' she started to cry. 'After Kia . . . there is no one else.'

She pulled back her hands and searched for a tissue. I waited, unsure of what to say.

'What about Dino?' I asked eventually.

She wiped her eyes. 'He says Prins wanted to leave me. That he was only using me for some business plan and has gone because it didn't work out. *I don't believe him.* Prins was never like that. He wouldn't break a promise . . .' She began to weep.

I put my arm around her to comfort her. She was rigid. 'He wouldn't,' she insisted. 'He wouldn't break a *promise.*'

When Mira came back home and found me sitting quietly with Lola, she rushed over, shrieking with surprise and hugged me tight. I was heartened to see that in marriage she had lost none of her vivacity. Her face looked a little stretched in places but, in my eyes, her every gesture still rippled with energy. In her fine white cotton with vermilion streaks she looked as strong and striking as ever, but when I asked her what she thought had happened to Prins, she burst into hot, harsh tears.

Her husband Ranil, who had followed her in, spoke for

her. His voice was grim. 'Nobody knows, *men*. Anything could have happened. You heard about Kia, no?'

I nodded, but said nothing. I heard Lola tear open another packet of tissues. I heard sobbing. I heard crows cawing outside. A dog baying.

O

The next day I went to find Dino at Bellevue. I felt I had to talk to him above the ground, even on his home territory, rather than beard him in his presidential bunker. I also wanted to feel the grit of the world Pearl, and then Prins, had conjured up for me. I wanted to look inside the Ducals' Arcadia just once; the house where Pearl had lived with Jason, and where Prins had been born. The place he wished to redeem with Lola.

I took a taxi but the driver had never heard of Bellevue: 'Bell *mokekdha*?' We stopped at a small drink-stall to ask the way. The man behind the row of blue and orange bottles spat out a slug of betel juice. 'Go straight, then turn this way and a bit to that side.' He moved his hand from side to side like fish heading upstream. 'You can't miss it.' He said the house is on its own. *The* house?

When we reached our destination there was no mistaking

it. Bellevue stood there in front of us: tall and stately and proud with acres of rubble around it, fenced in by a splattered line of white hoardings. Behind the façade dressed in filigree, its last walls were no more than a day away from the ball and chain of the giant crane poised over it, but it still looked huge and grand and desolate. Its garden, and the gardens of the houses in its ploughed-up wings, had been reduced to a sea of scalloped grey earth, a graveyard of incurable dreams.

As Lola had said, there was nothing left. Not for her, nor for Prins, nor for me. I could feel my resolve seep out and the questions I had for Dino evaporate. I wanted to live in hope as much as in truth.

In one corner of the vast plot of Vatunas land, on the footpath that would have once skirted Prins's home boundary, a large hoarding proclaimed the future: 'The New Arcadia'. The proposed flagship hotel of the Great Sands Corporation, the reconstituted hotel chain that Prins had worked for and Dino now ran, regenerating the whole of the Vatunases' land in its own name. There was an artist's futuristic drawing of an elegant garden hotel, shimmering in glass, with bougainvillea cascading over every recessed balcony and a column of starred features in bold red letters: air-conditioned honeymoon apartments, fantasy love suites, an Eros cinema and a subterranean ice rink with a Japanese snow machine. I stood in front of it waiting for Prins to

rise, bucking again, out of the disputed ground of his imagined world to free the future from the shadows of the past.
I wanted to hear him, or Pearl again, or the voice of the last
of her displaced dreamline, Dawn, spin us forward from
this hurt earth to a somehow better world.